THE BEAUTIFUL CHANGES

And yet, if a veil interposes between the shortsightedness of man and his future calamities, the same veil hides from him their alleviations; and a grief which had not been feared is met by consolations which had not been hoped.

THOMAS DE QUINCEY, *Confessions of an Opium-Eater*

the
beautiful
changes

Molly McCloskey

THE LILLIPUT PRESS
DUBLIN

First published 2002 by
THE LILLIPUT PRESS LTD
62–63 Sitric Road, Arbour Hill,
Dublin 7, Ireland
www.lilliputpress.ie

A CIP record for this title is available from
The British Library.

1 3 5 7 9 10 8 6 4 2

ISBN 1 901866 81 5

'Snow' was first published in *Force 10*. 'Dust' was first published in
Phoenix Irish Short Stories. 'Here, Now' was first published in Ger-
man as 'Hier, jetzt' in *Akzente*, and in English in *The Dublin Review*.
The author wishes to acknowledge the source of the title of this
book: Richard Wilbur's poem 'The Beautiful Changes', from *The
Beautiful Changes and Other Poems*, 1947.

*The Lilliput Press receives financial assistance from
An Chomhairle Ealaíon / The Arts Council of Ireland.*

Set in 10 on 15 Hoefler Text
Printed by ColourBooks, Baldoyle, Dublin

CONTENTS

The Beautiful Changes

7

Polygamy

147

Snow

169

Dust

187

Here, Now

205

The Beautiful Changes

Around the middle of that November, Henry's whole life fell away from him and in an absurdly graceful fashion. In a bar in Sacramento he had watched, as though it were the silent reel of a building being knocked by a wrecking ball, his destitute and sorry life crumble quietly but thoroughly before his eyes. And in the unheard din that reverberated, the breach between that moment and the next, what he saw in no particular shape was himself. It was him, it was certainly him, but without any thought or thing that had ever belonged to him, and what he was doing in the silence was calling to himself. He was calling himself home.

That the reel had reversed and his life, in all its ugly outmodedness, had risen up again and reassembled, didn't matter. What mattered was that he had seen, in the brief and sudden emptiness, himself, as yet unborn.

Which was why he was here doing what he was doing – shut up in the bedroom of a boarding house, with nothing to drink. Waking periodically, agitated and panic-stricken, thinking large chunks of his life had been stolen from him while he slept, only to find himself facing into night, when time would grind to a halt and he would wish for nothing but sleep. Nights he twitched through, pacing, communing with the pet sounds he'd once (cavalierly and while drunk and safely deaf to them) christened his *hoot owls*. Coos, whispers, susurrations. An animated, waking nightmare, with quick mutations of form and sudden quacking voice-overs.

When he dozed, finally, he would wake again startled, unsure whether the sickly yellow sky signalled the beginning or end of a day. That in-between time, when the air inside his room was a stricken mass of grey, unmoving grains: an ethereal grit that would either bleed together into blackness and night, or crystallize into recognizable forms: chair, table, bed and lamp advancing silently through the morning gloom.

He found it shocking that he should wake, and wake, and continue to wake, when there seemed nothing to wake for, and nothing he was doing to precipitate these repeated brushes with existence. As though there were a merciless persistence to life he would just have to outlast if he were to ... to what? Die? No, that wasn't what he'd locked himself in here to do, in fact the very opposite, he thought. He was here so as to live, wasn't he? But it was hard to keep it straight. That night, that night he'd known, it wasn't so very long ago – two, maybe three days, or was it only yesterday? – but how long could he live off that? Off a single moment of knowing. And in the midst of all this commotion (when it was enough to be getting from one minute to the next) it was hard to keep track of just what it was he had known. Like what exactly was he living *for*? This? No, he was living to feel *that* way again, the way he had that night. But who was to say, who knew if he'd ever feel that good again, he'd been drunk at the time anyway. So maybe that was it, maybe he was making a big mistake here, and the thing was not to survive this nightmare and come out the other side – an other side he wasn't even sure existed – but to be just a little bit drunk all the time. Why hadn't he thought of that before? But of course he had. Numerous times a day over the course of fifteen years, which meant that not only had he thought of it before, he had thought of it something like several thousand times.

Then one of those awful bouts of clarity would strike (a lucidity so keen and sharp he wouldn't dream of trusting it) and as though he were simply weekending in the country during unrelenting rains he would wonder idly, blankly, what to do with himself. He'd find himself sitting on the edge of the bed, his right leg slung over his left – wagging incessantly and at high speed – having briefly forgotten that he had just moments ago been weighing up the pros and cons of ending his life. And suddenly, it would broadside him – the possibility of ceasing to exist – and he would flinch in horror. In his mind then, he'd feel himself scurrying, madly, as he tried to get as far away as he could as fast as he could from that idea. He was like a spider racing around the sink, frantically fleeing its death, and why? It was always so sad to see – so heroic! – it had more than once moved him, watching some drab, uncelebrated, barely conscious creature summoning every bit of energy it had in a monumental effort to save its trivial life. And that was Henry, with about as much to go on.

The lucky thing about his fears was that they mutated, so that no single one of them managed to engulf him. Despite his near-paralysis, he felt at times wildly busy, a dozen narratives vying for his attention, as though he were watching several televisions simultaneously, all tuned to different stations. Under his feet, the dull brown carpet teemed, a sea of migratory ants, and across the room loose fibres from the armchair kinked ceiling-ward in hideous resolution, like the legs of insects under magnification.

Beyond the fibreboard wall, something long-nailed scuttled along the joists. He heard doors slam, keys turning in locks. His mother spoke to him.

He felt the room assume a lung-like quality. He had a sense of rhythmic swell and collapse. He was in a vacuum, clamped bug-like under glass, and what air he could breathe seemed frighteningly thin and he felt how precariously dependent he was on its supply. It was as though some lethal, undetected leak existed, and his eyes darted towards the ceiling in search of it, as if he might find it there and plug it. But what then? His supply would quickly dry up. Opening the door was not an option; he must ration. He pursed his lips and took small bird-like breaths which left him light-headed and panicky. And just when he was sure he would suffocate, the very room would inflate.

He slept on the floor. The unmade bed seemed swampy and a smell rose from it – unnervingly familiar – which agitated him, and of which he was obsessively aware. He stepped mindfully, anxiously, around the bed, as though he were an animal and it the corpse of some familiar fellow being.

Broad daylight and total darkness terrified him equally and he discovered ways of muffling each. In the morning, when the sun streamed through the thin brown curtains and made the flecked gold wallpaper spark, or in the evening, when the same sun ballooned a fierce yellow in his window, he stole the nubby spread from where it lay twisted at the end of the bed and tucked it up over the curtain rod. When night fell, he switched on the cheap desk lamp and bent its short spine-like neck so that its head drooped hangdog towards the floor, casting the minimum amount of light through the room. He lived then in degrees of grey, days and nights coming and going in a muted approximation of themselves.

Once or twice, something almost pleasant passed. Something that seemed like a mere memory revisited, a happy traipse through his past. His daughter, for instance, one summer's day, springing up at him from where she crouched hidden in the sand dunes.

Boo! he heard her cry. *Come'ere!*

And look! There she was! Jude. Having leapt from the shadows onto a velvety expanse of beach. Stretching out her hand to him – her hand! – her tanned summer hand with its coral-white nails, and he could nearly feel himself rising, going to her, letting her lead him – to where? – to the shoreline, to where the water would lap coolly up their bodies as they strode into the gentle breakers. But before he could reach her, the soft glow that had surrounded her became a brightness painful to behold, she acquired a glare, the glare of steel glinting in sunshine. He winced and the hallucination went haywire. The colours of it took on a hyperreal glow and seemed oddly disconnected from their objects. Her gleeful cries now a distant, haunting sing-song, looping through the room like a nursery rhyme distorted for effect.

He had rented this room in Sacramento about ten days before. Paid one month's rent and tucked his savings in an empty coffee can. It had seemed like a wad but when he'd counted it, it had been mostly ones, and had amounted only to $347.42, all that remained of his last brief bout of employment. For eight illusory weeks, he'd washed dishes in a Tex-Mex restaurant in Pismo Beach.

His boss, who was from Iowa or somewhere, ambled round to him at intervals and said things like, 'Hey amigo, watch the plates. They break ... *comprende?*' Masking his leeriness of Henry (for Henry had indeed grown frightening: more gaunt, it seemed, than anything that could support life) with a patronizing lift of his brows, he would call out, 'We need plates. *Rapido*. Whole ones.'

Before Henry had got the hang of their slippiness, he'd let two or three fall, creating beautiful white mosaics on the grey floor. He had gazed at them in shocked fascination, hypnotized by the echoes of shattering ceramic.

Nipping regularly from a flagon of vodka he kept tucked in his shoulder bag, Henry performed his duties in a soggy torpor. Sweat trickled down his arms and the small of his back and steam gushed at intervals from the large, continually humming dishwasher. Within this pocket of humidity, he felt dissociated from himself. He felt perched, as on a high shelf, watching himself move grimly and mechanically through the hot damp, both bewildered by the sight of himself and unable to believe that it was really himself he was seeing.

As for the others, they regarded him with a mixture of caution and pity which caused him to feel like some caged curiosity. They were equally unfathomable to him, and not only they, themselves, but the whole world in which they moved – their shared laughter, their rapid-fire talk, the mysterious enviable ease with which they inhabited themselves and the hours of their lives, a whole matrix of relations he couldn't begin to penetrate. Some invisible but undeniable field lay between him and them and he was torn between wanting, on the one hand, to be included, and, on the other, to take refuge in his exclusion. But it wasn't as though he had a choice. He didn't know how to be with people anymore, didn't know how to be in the world. And the world, it seemed, had nothing more to say to him.

He quit the job. Woke one morning and felt a near-total disconnection from the him who had for eight weeks sweated menially through that suffocating fog. He was at a complete loss as to how he could have dragged himself forth for as many mornings as he had. As for the necessary leaps – what would he do? where would money come from? how would he live? – he couldn't make them. Next month was a time he couldn't even conceive of, and tomorrow seemed hardly any closer.

After having made his way to Sacramento (for the ostensible but rather irrelevant reason of cities being meccas for opportunity), he had drunk most of his meagre savings in three or four dark bars there, then found himself early one evening sitting sipping Scotch in a place called Alfie's, looking at his life as idly and as dispassionately as if it were a piece of street theatre he'd stumbled on and from which he would, as easily, walk away. And that was when it had fallen from view – his life – and left him with a calm the likes of which he'd never felt before, save perhaps on one occasion, the occasion of his very first drink. In this blank space there was neither the frantic anticipation of impending drunkenness nor that sense of hovering doom which had grown so constant as to be practically companionable. There was only his self, free of any future or the fear of it (which by now were one and the same) and unburdened by the weight of his past.

He'd sat there at his corner table, peering intently but distractedly into the semi-dark, like someone trying to hear better. Either he had reached a pitch of perfect alcoholic detachment, so far gone that the details of his life finally had ceased to bother him, or he had seen meaning. He had seen beyond the grim particulars and behind them he had found this thing – could he call it a thing? – this calm, this space, that seemed to be waiting for him, in fact to have been waiting for a long time. He couldn't touch it, that much he knew. Couldn't get at or change or destroy it, not fully, because in a funny way it wasn't just his, this thing. This thing, this thing, his soul, why couldn't he just say it? Yes, that was it, he imagined he had seen his soul! But not just his. It was outside of him too, like a gift being passed between pairs of hands, arrested in the act of being given. To remain forever half his, half not.

It passed, the moment passed, and his life crowded in on him again. He became aware of a sensation that felt a little like grime forming, though it was nothing more than the return of his familiar swarm of thoughts. What he imagined he'd seen, there in that slim space of calm – cracked like a door he could not quite slip through – was the place where all this would be over. Where he would do the things that normal people did and feel all the time the way he had just then, when the filth had peeled away and something fine and undefiled had been revealed behind it.

The longing to be sober gripped him like a yearning for some imagined homeland. Sober, he thought, he would catch trains and be home nights and eat eggs for breakfast. He would garden, tend flowers, doze under a ripe autumnal sun. He would take brisk morning walks, bound manfully up the steps of his house, drink coffee in a kitchen awash with sunlight. He would sit beside a hearth, read real books, write letters, talk on the telephone, slap his thigh with mirth. What a happy man he'd be! When he worked, he'd whistle, and even if he was alone he'd be OK. And best of all, best of all he wouldn't shake. He would never, ever shake.

He had a drink in his hand, he had a Scotch. Oh the old tricks he'd come to loathe. For how many times had he contemplated the thrills of abstinence from the safe perch of drunkenness? This cheap armchair sobriety. Box seats at the flip side of his life. Sitting there drinking, imagining not drinking, saying to himself: *I could do that*.

It bored him sick.

He didn't know what time he'd left Alfie's. He'd sat there drinking Scotch, his dreams of a bright and sober future growing fuzzier and impossible to follow. From one moment to the next, he would forget what it was he'd been thinking. It seemed that something had made him feel intensely good, but already he could not be sure what it had been and he had trouble believing it had been anything at all. Now, he felt himself drowning, and the few faces left in the bar looked smeared, as though immersed in murky water. Dead-eyed, dumb, they seemed to stall in front of him, then dart past, fish-like. The space above him pressed down upon him and his head drooped under the weight of this imagined water. What Henry didn't realize was that he was weeping.

The next thing he was aware of was lying curled on the floor of his room, wide-eyed, with the side of his head pressed to the floor, as though eavesdropping on the room below. He had, almost immediately on waking, that familiar sensation that the incidents of the previous night had sneakily assembled while he slept – an unruly and dishevelled throng of events all clamouring for his attention. It was like finding himself suddenly surrounded by a crowd of street urchins who had somehow learned his name.

He sat up, clutching his shins, rocking back and forth on his haunches. He felt the sucked-in concavity of his belly and the jut of his knees against his chin. His organs called attention to themselves in a way that horrified him. Something like his stomach or intestines was buckling in an attempt to reshuffle its non-existent contents. His blood-flow was too close to the surface of his thin skin, and his heart throbbed with such force he worried it would burst its walls. He felt too frail to sustain the violence of his own vital functions. The room had by then begun to breathe, swelling and retracting, and out of the corners of his eyes he saw figures dart and zing. Little sizzled hairs danced across his field of vision and a painful pulling sensation accompanied each pendulous swing of his eyes. In the far reaches of his hearing, he could detect the beginnings of an ominous din, as though of distant march music drawing nearer. He felt himself growing smaller at its approach. He watched himself shrinking, cartoonishly so. He was so tiny – what was he doing? – why he was teetering on the lip of a bottle of Scotch. He was the size of his own thumbnail. How did I get so small, he wondered – and then plop, he saw himself fall in. And this time, he knew that he was weeping.

For years Jude has been trying to come to some sort of an arrangement with reality. She couldn't say exactly when it started, this jockeying for position in her own life, this quest for a vantage point from which the events of each day would cohere into a kind of harmony – something like an airplane passenger's view of things, she thought, when the world would grow quaintly inter-locking right under her eyes and she could sit back and survey things into sense. By the time she was twelve, a degree of chaos had entered her life. She found herself in silent, uneasy collusion with the adult world on such subjects as desire, and her father's increasingly erratic mood swings and intermittent disappear-ances made him seem like something moving in and out of focus.

She loved him. And in strange new ways. She coveted his com-pany; she felt an intense and helpless desire to be near him. She was fascinated by the breadth of his thighs, the roll of his strong shoulders, by the effusion of hair that ranged wildly across his chest and down his dark torso, eddying in unruly swirls, produc-ing in her a slight and delicious fear of she didn't know what (but how dissimilar he was to the boys she knew, with their baby-smooth stick limbs and their little pink dabs of nipples). Being alone with him in the car, or walking with linked arms, she had her first real taste not only of desire, but of conquest and completion. Sitting beside him, alone, she felt the thrill of possession, sensed the sway she held over him, and revelled, with a certain incongruous pride (for he was by then a sometimes difficult drunk), in her own primacy of place in his world; he was, after all, the only man to whom she would ever be literally irreplaceable. At the best of times – those occasions on which he was his old exuberant and attentive self – she experienced her first intimations of what it was to be in love. And yet in spite of this new and desperate closeness, she could feel him slipping from her. The more she yearned for him, the more elusive he seemed to grow until it became clear that she had grossly overestimated her own power. She was no longer always able to reach him or console him or be consoled by him, and she sensed, without being fully conscious of just what it would mean, that she was losing him.

In the face of this growing confusion, she had the desire not to disappear or die (as several of her friends, for their own reasons, claimed to have); she didn't dream of hopping a freight train or joining the circus or even being adopted by the Kennedys. No, she wanted to remain true to her own reality and yet somehow rise above it, transcend its frustrating particulars and, from her new position of magical omnipotence, minister to its needs. The night she saw *Our Town* on television, she imagined she had found the means.

It was the version in which Emily – faithful to the text – is allowed to die, and Jude was captivated by the sight of Emily and all her dead companions up there in the hilltop cemetery watching over the living, over their breakfast tables and their weddings, their bungled attempts at kindness or their heedless disregard, all the little things they did that they didn't even notice because they were alive and too busy doing them.

Oh, Mother Gibbs, I never realized before how troubled and how – how in the dark live persons are … From morning till night, that's all they are – troubled.

She recognized herself in the character of Emily and along with Emily cursed the blithe inattentiveness of the living, deciding then and there that she would no longer collude in such neglect; she would take nothing for granted, she would stop sleepwalking her way through life and she would wake her whole family while she was at it. The thought of her project made her intensely happy.

After that, Jude tried hard – if briefly – to weight each meaningless moment or offhanded gesture with the significance it deserved. In class, she cocked her head to one side and smiled beatifically at her classmates; at the dinner table, she felt imbued with a lofty responsibility, because neither her father nor her mother – nor Bill, certainly – seemed to realize that this was it – life! – this very moment. She stared at the three of them in turn – shovelling food into their mouths, chewing vacantly, her father taking a slug from his beer and winking swim-eyed at her, her mother smoothing down the already smooth gingham (gingham!) tablecloth – until her mother said:

'Jude, what's wrong?'

'Nothing's wrong.'

'Then why aren't you eating? Why are you squinting like that?'

She hadn't realized she'd been squinting.

'I'm pretending I'm dead,' she said.

'What?'

'Oh thank god,' Bill said.

Her father stopped chewing and stared at her intently

Though she wasn't sure why, she could see he was pleased. Yes, pleased with her. She had struck that mysterious chord in him that she could not name but had been ever adept at locating.

She smiled at him as if to say, At least someone understands.

'Proceed,' she said, motioning towards their plates. 'Please.'

'Pro*ceed*,' Bill said.

Her mother looked gravely at her. 'But why, dear?' she asked. 'Why do you want to be dead?'

'I don't want to *be* dead,' Jude said, rolling her eyes. 'I just want to see things like I'm dead –'

Bill emitted a macaroni-strangled noise which was intended to sound like a schlock horror scene of someone being buried alive.

'– so I won't take them for granted.'

'That's impressive,' her father said, sounding to her disappointingly unimpressed.

'Yes,' she said solemnly, 'I'm sure it's working.'

But it wasn't working. No matter how often she said: I will spend one hour each day being dead, or ten minutes each hour, or during commercial breaks only, it didn't work. Sometimes she forgot she was dead or, if she remembered, what she saw when she looked at her parents in that way seemed to cast them, if anything, in a less favourable light. Instead of feeling moved by the sweet trivia of their lives, she felt disheartened by their almost doltish way of barrelling through the day. She began to suspect that there was a reason we did not subject one another to such scrutiny: people just didn't bear up well under it.

Her failure in this project left her sadly disappointed in herself and led her to conclude that it was not possible to be fully alive and fully aware of the miracle of being alive at the same time. Since she was only twelve, she did not put it quite like that.

She may not have put it any way at all. In fact, she probably just gave up and forgot.

Until, that is, she saw that program on Confucius, who when asked about enlightenment apparently had said: *When I eat, I eat; when I sleep, I sleep.* Or something like that. Now there was the perfect recipe for living, the answer she'd been waiting for, and she vowed then and there that she would live fully – be in each and every moment rather than above it, have what she had while she still had it, and infect the rest of them with this grand appreciation for the wonder of the present.

Her every move (or as often as she remembered) assumed a bathetic intensity she hoped would not go unnoticed, though she'd gathered from watching that program that such a desire for recognition was somehow counter to the very concept of enlightenment. Nevertheless she was delighted when her parents appeared somewhat bewildered, even awe-struck, by the change in her. She imagined them wondering if perhaps she was one of those spiritual child prodigies whose premature wisdom they would humbly and gratefully bow to. When her father nipped off to the Quik-mart for a bottle of something, she threw her arms around him.

'Good bye, Father,' she cried, one fist clenched over her heart.

'Father?'

'Live each moment as though it were your last,' she called.

'Will do, honey.'

It occurred to her a few years later that if she hadn't been so busy refusing to consider life beyond the present moment, she might have recognized a certain finality in one of those departures and, if not prevented it from occurring, at least made clear to him that she was not so enlightened as to be beyond needing him. But whether out of her muddled Confucianism, or because of the deceptive nonchalance with which he made his actual departure, it was with the same intense carelessness that she bade him goodbye when he left for the last time.

He was always waiting. Waiting for his life to begin, or begin again. For tomorrow to be different, for the past to reinstate itself, for a brand-new naïveté to wipe everything he'd learned away. He waited for morning, evening, darkness, sleep, for a permanent abeyance of panic. He waited for opening time, closing time, a moment that would alter the course of his life.

Over time, Henry had developed an unshakeable belief (if you could use the word belief to signify such a passive, cowering anticipation) in some vague but inevitable doom, and he waited for that, sometimes without even knowing he was. No amount of reasoning with himself (what doom? how would it befall him? had it not failed to materialize thus far?) could succeed, for any length of time, in seriously lessening his dread.

Being drunk helped. When Henry was very drunk, he wasn't conscious of anything, even of waiting. But when he was just drinking, just drinking and not yet drunk, then he could feel himself – half there and with one eye trained on something in the mental middle distance – waiting, anxiously, for what felt like the next drink. Even when he was sitting in a bar with plenty of money in his pocket and more liquor in the place than he could drink in a week, even when there was no danger of the next drink not arriving, still he waited.

How mistaken people were in thinking that a drunk, once he had a drink in his hand, was relaxed! When, really, some little part of him was always on red alert. At how many parties, in the long ago, had Henry risen from his slumped torpor on the sofa – a slumbering giant suddenly all business, suddenly the unbending bureaucrat – and, as though informed by a sixth sense as to the state of his supply, announced, with an incontestable and grave authority, that the liquor store would be closing in ten minutes? How many times, while asleep (or so it had seemed) at the bar, had he lifted his head at ten minutes to two – as though there existed in his brain a special receptor which never slept and which was invested with the sole responsibility of registering the words *last call* – and ordered another drink?

He knew there would always be alcohol. And yet the knowledge did nothing to quell this vague impatience. So it couldn't be that, could it, the thing he was waiting for? No, deep down, he knew that what he was really waiting for was something beyond the next drink, or even the next one after that; he was waiting for a different moment altogether, the moment when finally, mysteriously, miraculously, he would have had *enough* to drink.

He can remember, years ago, actually picturing himself at some future dinner party, one hand placed protectively – almost affectionately – over the rim of his empty wine glass, announcing blithely, *Oh, none for me, I don't bother with the stuff anymore!*

Yes, he used to see himself jovial, self-possessed, aglow with a kind of knowing tranquillity, for he was a man who knew when to leave folly behind; there was a time for drink and a time to be sober, and in knowing that, he was wiser than most. When others marvelled at his equanimity, his serene, poised, sober, but by no means dull countenance (oh the fun he could have without it, even as all around him others grew dull-witted, repetitive, garbled, prostrate), he would, with a nonchalance they could only admire, and a delicate wave of his hand, say, *I just sort of ... grew out of it, you know.*

And yet the closer it seemed he should have been coming to such a time – the time when he would finally be sated – the less he was able to imagine not wanting it. He could see all around him people who didn't drink as much or as eagerly as he did. Moderate drinkers, they were called. They drank socially, normally, wisely. They knew their limits. But these people – with their never-exceeded two cocktails, their grating stupidity after half a bottle of wine, their way of switching to water just as things were getting interesting (this *interruptus* that was to him unfathomable) – struck him as sub-human. He imagined that in their temperance, with their mediocre and easily met appetites, they must be miserable, certainly more miserable than he, with his abundance of appetite, though perhaps they didn't know they were only half alive, which accounted for their not being bothered by the fact.

Teetotallers, on the other hand, he found infinitely more interesting, though he took care to keep them at a distance. They appeared to him a strange breed of ghost: if moderate drinkers seemed never to have been alive, then dry drunks existed in a kind of eerie afterlife. They knew too much, and seemed rather poignantly burdened by it all, enveloped in an almost gracious pathos.

Nevertheless, this word *enough*, which he repeated incessantly, helplessly, as though believing if only he could sound the right note, he would produce the desired effect:

That's enough now.

One more, I haven't had enough.

You've had enough.

Enough, enough, what is enough?

Alright now, enough is enough.

And sometimes, from just within earshot: *He's had enough*.

And yet he knew better than anyone that he had not had near enough. Because the more he drank, the greater became his need, and the more pressing the need, the less of himself he seemed able to bring to the occasion, until finally, no matter how much he drank, he experienced himself as an increasingly empty vessel. Without idea or opinion or passion – a dull, parasitic guest at life's table, with never enough nobility to leave.

And to think there was a time it had completed him. The night of his very first drink, he'd been gripped by an uncanny sense of reunion, as though two halves of him had been – unbeknownst to him until then – lost to one another; in the initial, restful flush of inebriation, he had the feeling not so much that he'd discovered something new as the feeling that something finally had been returned to him. His vague yearnings seemed suddenly justified. So this, he thought, is the person I was meant to be.

When had it begun, exactly? He used to love his life, didn't he? He used to love life. When he was a boy of six or seven, summer mornings of pale blue skies and birdsong. It was nothing for Henry to be up at dawn, he was never a sleeper, not at that age. Look at all there was to do, and see! He was greedy in a way his father said would serve him well. 'You expect a lot,' he told him, 'and that probably means you'll get it.'

He used to walk his father to the mines some mornings, the

swallows singing and Henry feeling so light he felt he'd float away. He held his father's black lunch pail in one hand, knocking it against his knee as he march-stepped. His other hand curled in his father's. Ahead of them in the distance, the low blue hills, velvety and looking small enough to stroke. And then he'd leave his father at the gate after their obligatory, almost parodic exchange.

'Bring me with you.'

'You know that's not allowed.'

'When can I then?'

'Never, I hope.'

'But I want to.'

'You don't.'

'I do.'

'Well, you don't make the rules.'

Down on one knee then, in genuflection, his father bidding him goodbye. As he turned towards the mine, towards the black shaft – that door that rose right out of the earth, a door to nowhere at all – Henry would crane his neck after him, as though his father were a letter he'd mailed. And later, at dinner time, waiting for him to arrive home again, his father's appearance each evening as miraculous to Henry as a letter that, having passed through so many hands, still managed to reach him.

Wasn't he happy then? Wasn't everything still undecided? He has to believe it was, otherwise that boy was only passing time until his life took its inevitable, unfortunate shape. How sad he feels for him! As though the boy were his own son, someone he'd let horribly down. He sees a small form lying in bed at night after ball games, eleven or twelve years old, fingering his raw thighs – burns from sliding into base. He sees him sitting in the dugout, staring fascinated as (with a deliberate slowness and such a look of ceremony it seemed a symphony should accompany their emergence) beads of blood materialized on the surface of his skin, leaving his thigh peppered with a profusion of tiny scabs, battle scars he stroked under the sheets at night, reliving his performance.

Blood again, but this time hers. She was his first lover, the year before they were married, there in that summer house her cousins had rented, in broad daylight and with the sea breeze puffing the thin white curtains. Afterwards, her own thighs smeared with blood. He'd been astonished by how much of it there was, neither of them knowing whether or not to be alarmed. He'd pressed his thumb in it, transfixed by the sight of his faint red fingerprint on her skin. So happy, it scared him. His life too good to be true.

Henry was working his way up through the minors by then and every day was like the happiest day of his childhood. Everybody said the same thing about him: he was heading for the majors and he was going to be big. But he'd had some bad luck. There'd been that business with his arm. Adhesions on the elbow, he'd never even heard the word. The pain was excruciating, a terrible burning sensation he tried his best to ignore. They told him he could pitch his way out of it, work his way right through it till it loosened up and disappeared, as though it were nothing more than a little muscle stiffness. And the next thing he knew it was over, not the pain but his career. Four years and seven months of uninterrupted progress, and within a couple of weeks it was all behind him. At the end he'd become a laughing-stock, each crack of a bat connecting like a gong announcing his failure. Rich, resonant *crack*. He used to hear that sound in his sleep, used to dream base hits whizzing past his nose, cruel laughter reverberating from an unseen periphery, the muddled echo of the actual humiliation he'd heard raining on him from the stands.

'You're a bum, Henry,' they yelled. 'Go home to your mother.'

'Go home to your grandmother, Henry!'

'Take a hike, candy ass!'

'My grandmother's pitching relief today.'

Icing his elbow that last night, Mo told him she didn't care if he pumped gas for a living, as long as he loved her. He didn't know if it was true, but he also didn't think it would ever come to that. He'd looked up at her from the kitchen chair, doe-eyed with pain and devastation, and she'd cradled his head like a child's.

All that summer he'd been out of a job, still reeling from the injustice of it all. And that was the summer he developed a taste for flight, a few times taking off at night, driving down the turnpike to the shore, a bottle wedged between his thighs. Could he ever describe to anyone or even to himself the absolute sufficiency of setting out alone with a full quart and hours stretching ahead of him? He needed nothing other than what he had: drink, solitude, movement and a destination.

In the middle of the night he would spread his jacket on the sand and watch the waves roll in. It was a kind of gentle delirium then, a liquid joy, a comfort nearly amniotic in its envelopment and lull; he sat cradled in the darkness, hearing only the rhythmic muffled clap of water meeting water and the sloshing *glunk* of whiskey as it rushed to meet his lips.

He fancied he was drunk on joy as much as anything. He felt rich with things – intelligence, wisdom, perception, sensitivity. The limits, the doubts, the petty fears had evaporated and he swam in a kind of glorious certainty, a sea of sympathy and good intention, in love with all humanity. And he was sure then that this glimpse of how things really stood was there all the time, just waiting for him. The unintoxicated eye was hooked on sterility, habituated to its unhappy vantage point, but that unhappiness

could vanish, he discovered, and when it did what abiding wonder was revealed beyond! In the midst of such transcendence, his
everyday mind appeared pitiable and uncomprehending and he
felt himself a god, gazing down paternally on the child who was
also him, but sober.

He'd started blacking out.

Once, after one of those midnight reveries on the beach, he'd
found himself standing in front of the house in which, six years
earlier, he and Mo had made love for the first time. Nobody lived
there, just a succession of summer tenants, a stream of anony-
mous visitors who didn't even know he and Mo existed, let alone
had loved each other there. He stood in the dark, beside the
hedge that rimmed the lawn, staring at the house and saddened
by the fact that such moments in his life could dissolve like that
into nothing. Everything was change, transience. He was twenty-
four, but felt ancient, already looking back and wondering: will it
ever be that good again?

Half stumbling, half tiptoeing around the perimeter of the
house, he groped his way along the outer walls and shrubs and
drainpipes, making his way to the window of the bedroom – their
bedroom – a strange excitement rising in him. Oh this was fun,
he thought, this was really rather thrilling, he was like a member
of a SWAT team in the midst of a hostage drama. Climbing on a
deck chair he'd picked up along the way, he grasped the ledge of
the window. He had to stand on the arm of the chair in order to
see in and when his eyes crested the sill a funny half-sick sensation came over him, the kind that comes with spying strangers'
bodies under bedclothes, muted shapes shifting with eerie innocence in their sleep. He bit his lip, the chair buckled underneath
him, its arm knocked loudly against the side of the house and the
back yard was awash in light, lights were flicking on inside, one

by one, in a silent, xylophonic *binkboopbong* until the entire house blazed.

He dismounted, capsizing the deck chair as he did. In panicked retreat, he trampled brutally on several clusters of lovingly set pansies, for which he felt a momentary but real stab of sorrow, and then hit the side of his head on the corner wall of the house as he was looking backward and hurrying forward at the same time.

He scampered down the street and with shaking hands fumbled the keys into the ignition. Not daring to turn the headlights on, he drove creepingly away, his head drooping, his shoulders hunched, slinking out of town under a cloud of suspicion. Oh what was he doing? This was the kind of thing people got arrested for. He pictured himself behind bars, *Pervert* spray-painted across his front door.

The following day she'd told him. He was sitting, ceremoniously circling the want ads and sipping – with an exaggerated disinterest he didn't at all feel – a beer, when she sat down beside him and said, 'I'm pregnant.'

'Pregnant,' he repeated. 'You're *pregnant?*'

When the shock had subsided, he felt delighted, both by the idea of a baby, and by the fact that her announcement bumped them out of last night's groove and justified – no, demanded! – a celebration. He was taken aback at how quickly the word *pregnant* had – by a sequence of non-verbal associations – led him to the word *champagne*. He made a quick trip to the liquor store and he and Mo spent a quiet evening cooing over impending parenthood, the champagne – and the vision of himself with the flute perched atop his knee – restoring him not only to physiological equilibrium, but also to a more palatable version of himself. It

33

was a lesson he remembered. In years to come, whenever he felt particularly sordid or ignoble or ridiculous, he would, if he could, buy champagne. There was a kind of self-fulfilling prophecy inherent in the act: he was a man drinking champagne, therefore he must be a man who was entitled to be drinking champagne.

He'd gotten a job, and it wasn't pumping gas. It was covering baseball for the *Philadelphia Daily News*. It was odd at first, this funny mix of emasculation and power – watching from the press box and knowing he could've done it better himself and yet finding in it all, in being the eyes and ears of a whole city, a kind of addictive pleasure too.

When the others went home for the day, he leaned back in his chair, lit a cigarette and openly admired his byline. Along with this taste of omnipotence (for it was he who had determined what was known about a given thing), he felt a real and tender satisfaction with himself. He tilted his head to one side, looked at the stack of reporter's notebooks on his desk and thought about his life these last couple of months. He shook his head affectionately at his own excesses, as though they'd been of the heart, a mad love affair over which he'd briefly been a fool. He'd been a bit intemperate, it was true, he'd drunk much too much, but that was one of the drawbacks to having a character like his – passionate, intense, driven! You took things hard, you went too far at times. And wasn't it better, he thought, to be overly alive and suffer for it than to sleepwalk through life, safely aloof to its extremes? But just look at him now. How dependable he could be when necessary and what a peculiar joy he felt in being so.

Three years later, it all imploded. Called into the editor's office (pigeon-chested man named Kohler who'd probably never seen the inside of a dugout) and accused of scrambling a few details of a Phillies-Pirates double-header, events from the fourth inning of the second game he'd attributed to the third of the first, or something like that. And what was worse he'd apparently mis-quoted someone, absurdly so, he gathered.

'And you know, Henry, this isn't the first time this has come up.'

'People don't remember what they say. You know that.'

'Maybe *you* don't remember what they say.'

He looked at the wall.

'If you could ... do something about it, we could reconsider your position, Henry, but as it is, you've become a liability.'

A liability? He couldn't believe what he was hearing. 'Do something ... about what exactly?'

'Oh come on, Henry. You know as well as I do.' His raised hand held an imaginary glass and he made two quick flicking motions in the direction of his mouth. 'Look, you go away, you make some changes, we'll talk. I like you Henry, I do, you know that. I remember you' – he wagged his finger – 'you had a future out there. And you got a raw deal. But I can't have it, I just can't have it. One of these days I'm liable to get my ass sued, and *then* who'll be out of a job?'

'But, I don't understand. What are you saying? Exactly.'

'I'm saying that as things stand I have to let you go.'

He sat at the bar in shock. Go away and make some changes? He knew what that meant. He was supposed to stop drinking. Stop? He was twenty-seven years old. Maybe when he was thirty-seven, or forty-seven, yes, then it would fine, it might even be right, drinking was a young man's game after all, but now? He flagged the bartender. A liability! He could run rings around any of those dopes in his department, he was in a different league altogether, he wasn't just reporting – recounting events – he was creating! Whole worlds, atmospheres, the pathos of defeat and the banal triumphalism of victory. There was a time he thought he'd get his own column, he'd been on the verge of it, in fact, there had been discussions, and then from somewhere in the invisible echelons of upper management had come the decision: the time 'just wasn't right'. How they'd miss him now. How his readers would complain. *Mellifluous*, one of them had written, in a brief, unforgettable paean that had appeared on the letters page, *a mellifluous style*. Mellifluous styles didn't grow on trees, you didn't get mellifluous from every two-bit amateur just up from the *Bumfuck Tribune*. And anyway, if you were as good as he was, they had to expect you to be a little off your nut. One night working late, after filing copy, standing on top of his desk, singing *I gotta be me*. Well what about it? What ever happened to the days of hard-drinking hacks, whiskey bottles in the desk drawers, a little nip-nip to keep you fuelled at deadline?

He didn't know what to do. He didn't know how to do anything else. He called for another whiskey and ordered himself to stay calm. Perhaps ... perhaps he could make a comeback. Yes, that's what he would do, get another job at another paper and arise triumphant, vindicated. One morning Kohler would pick up the sports page and find Henry covering the Series for the competition. Special emphasis on the inner turmoil that came with high-level competition, the nervous sickness you never saw, the bizarre pre-game rituals, the superstitions peculiar to the stars, an insider's view of the pressure-cooker. He imagined himself up for a Pulitzer, sportswriters didn't often win Pulitzers but then he wasn't just any sportswriter. Yes, this could be a blessing in disguise, he'd probably been selling himself short at that rag anyway. Suddenly, he knew what he would do. He'd go home, regroup, and map his comeback.

He hadn't made a comeback, and it hadn't been a blessing in disguise. He'd gotten another job alright, exactly like he'd said he would. It just wasn't a job they gave Pulitzers for.

'Hardware?'

'You'd be surprised at the money that's in it.'

'But why me?' Henry asked. 'I don't know hardware.'

'I remember you,' Jed said. 'How could I forget?' He remembered him from his baseball days (but not from his years at the *Daily News*, Henry puzzled, didn't people read?). In fact Jed's son had come up alongside Henry in the minors and was now shagging flies first-string for the Cardinals.

'That's your son?'

'Sure is,' Jed said. 'Anyway, I'm getting older. And I'm not going to keep this up forever. And my son, well, he's certainly not about to take up the reins.'

'No, I imagine he's busy.'

'So I thought maybe you could buy in and who knows? When the time comes, all going well, it'd be yours.'

Two weeks later he was standing behind the counter in Narberth Hardware, unsure if he should laugh or cry. (And this was where things grew murky, where the line between possibility and its absence began to blur, so that he found himself asking: How did this happen? How did I get here?)

He treated his new career in hardware as though it were a rather awkward adolescent phase he could later deny having passed through. If, in the beginning, he ever did find himself content, or at least forgetting his vow of discontent, he checked himself. And if he ever whistled while he worked, it was only to show his mind was elsewhere. He was slumming it, seeing how the other half lived, the half with small, mildly embarrassing dreams. Henry wasn't destined for such provincial mediocrity. He took the job alright, but with an air of standing in for someone else. And he busied himself at once cultivating a distance from his own life.

She was twelve and they were at a rental house down at the shore and he was dancing on the table top.

'C'mon Judy! Get up here! I can't do this alone!'

The sweat gleamed on his forehead and his madness was infectious. She made a self-conscious but prolonged attempt at mirroring his movements, twisting on the ball of one foot, her other leg jackknifing at a forty-five-degree angle. It made her think of a dog urinating on a fire hydrant and she felt ridiculous, but he cheered her on.

'That's my girl,' he cried breathlessly, 'that's my lady!'

Where was Bill? Nowhere to be seen. Holed up in his room, probably, reading filched copies of Harold Robbins, dirty parts only. Or working his first job, washing dishes at a burger place on the boardwalk. He told her later, very straight-faced, that it was the summer he became a man.

'Whatever do you mean, my dear?' she'd asked, fidgeting.

'It was when I realized everything was kaput. Even more kaput than I'd thought. I sort of knew then that he'd be leaving.'

'You did?'

'Wasn't it obvious?'

'Well ... I don't know. I thought he was still OK then –'

'OK? Are you kidding? He was out of his tree. Don't you remember?'

She remembers, yes. She just hadn't known what it meant. How had Bill known? He was a year younger than she was. Of course she never admitted to Bill how even when Henry packed his few bags and said *I have to go away for awhile* she really thought awhile meant awhile. For months, she'd believed he was coming back, simply because it was unbelievable that he wouldn't. It wasn't even a matter of convincing herself, she just knew. He might leave Bill, he might even leave her mother, but he couldn't leave her. She knew him better than that. But as it turned out, she didn't know him. It was Bill who'd known him, who'd known what he was going to do even before he did it. He was out of his tree.

And her mother, where was her mother when they were twisting on the table top? She sometimes seemed to tag along, or perhaps be dragged along, on nights like that. But eventually, and Jude could sometimes feel it coming, her mother would assume a stern or dismissive air and retreat to the kitchen or the den, distancing herself from the proceedings in a way that left Jude feeling implicated in whatever crime her father was committing. Jude inevitably sided with him; it was always more fun. At the decisive sound of some door closing, he would raise his eyebrows and shrug and she would mimic his expression, the delicious sense of having conspired with him in some mutinous act tempered by a guilty suspicion that she had, somehow, sold out.

And how many next mornings she had seen, merging for her as surely as they did for him, the solemnity of his hangovers in inverse proportion to the madness of the previous night. In time she became so practised at assessing his degree of pain, she needn't have been privy to last night's fun in order to deduce roughly what his state of mind had been.

He lay in his room in the cool summer dark. With his frayed nerves and near-death demeanour, both sterile- and sickly-smelling, he reminded her of science lab, of things pickled and unnaturally preserved. He withdrew from her those mornings, his absence worse because it came in the wake of such apparent intimacy. In his drunkenness, he'd been utterly available. Had joined her in her child's world of spontaneity and minor hell-raising. Had offered her his best self, only to snatch it back the following morning, leaving her wondering (however inarticulately) whether the previous night's sympathy, its delirious rapport, had not been all in her imagination.

What she regretted then (just as he did) was not the delirium, not the mania itself, but the fact that such happiness had to end so sadly.

The word *hangover*. Which made her think of a man in a movie dangling, in quasi-comic peril, from a branch jutting out of a rock face. Hangover: the word itself so burdened with mystery and shifting registers and its own day-to-day existence that it had come to acquire a nearly human form. Lumbering dolefully about the house – oversized outcast, mute with inexpressible pain – or lounging brashly when so aggrieved as to be beyond caring about offence. Attendant in attitudes of silence, or servility, or sickness, but, strangely, most oppressively present when hidden from view, as when her father did not emerge from his bedroom until late morning, long after her own day had commenced, and her first glimpse of him would be when he came ambling down the sand towards their little beach encampment.

She would think, almost automatically then, of the previous night, of how he'd twirled in darkness on the wooden deck, perhaps, palms facing up and eyes to the heavens, as though snowflakes were falling from on high. And seeing him those mid-afternoons – a beach chair hanging from one hand, a can of Budweiser clutched in the other – she felt as though a second day were getting underway. For she associated (semi-consciously, much as she might have the early-morning smell of frying bacon) the sight of that can with another day having officially dawned.

Bill would not acknowledge his arrival. They had reached the point of being practically invisible to one another. Bill had a girlfriend that summer, his first. A rather mangy-looking brown-skinned blonde who would migrate from her own family's encampment in order to share lunch with them on the beach. The blonde and Bill chewing purposefully through their sandwiches, their legs stretched straight out in front of them, their four knobby knees in a row, too shy to say much in front of the others. But when they walked towards the shoreline, Jude could see them chattering away quite seriously, quite agreeably, their heads inclined and their hands locked behind their own backs, like little diplomats emerging from negotiations.

She remembers her father having lifted his head from the *Inquirer* long enough to mumble to her mother: *He's human after all.*

'Human,' Jude repeated, lifting her own head from her fanzine, sensing in the current climate of what sounded like the mild denigration of her brother the possibility of compliments being bestowed on her. 'And am I human?' she asked.

Her mother smiled, but continued to gaze towards the shoreline. Abstractions were mostly his department.

'You, dear,' her father said, 'are all too human.'

Henry has never seen such rain. Every kind of sky seems capable of disgorging it and no time of day refuses it. It moves down his street in flat wide sheets that make him think of an army advancing in waves. It gushes, sporadically, from roof gutters, teems in sleet-cold needles that sting his skin. On the most blustery days he has even seen it raining upwards, freak gusts of air catching the droplets and yanking them heavenward. But what he most loves (for Henry does love the rain) is when the sun shines through it so that the earth glistens, as though smeared in its own juices.

These days, Jean often finds him on the fronch porch, bundled up against the cold, staring at a drizzle so constant it seems stationary.

'It's possible you're deep in thought,' she says, 'but I'm afraid you're just getting depressed by the weather.'

The weather. They speak of it here with a mixture of awe and intimacy and seem to survive it through the continuous cutting of deals. They can't ignore it, but neither can they let it get the better of them, so they pay a sort of lip service to its depressive powers. Strangely, Henry thinks, they are grateful to it too, precisely because of its hardship, grateful for the chance to prove their mettle.

He can't explain it to her, how he finds rain a comfort. The heavens' relentless cleansing of the earth like the flushing out of a new wound. The way nothing stands absolutely still. Even in the woods, he feels the air stir, wind slipping through chinks in the tree line. The high broad leaves thrumming quietly under the drumbeat of rain; water gathering and dropping, then gathering and dropping again so that low to the ground, ferns quiver under second- or third-hand rain. Overhead, the clouds amass and roll in great migrations, while at his feet, dead trees teem with bug-life. Innumerable shades of green, seeming always to be greater or lesser versions of one another, pass by like stages in the evolution of the colour.

Henry feels a hum from the earth, as though it were at all times ministering to itself. He thinks of a beehive, hidden worlds of minute transformation, the word *digestion*. And yet in spite of all this – this movement, motion, this churning and stirring – there exists a convalescent hush he has never felt in any other place.

He is subject also to an odd, disarming sadness. Sober, he feels suddenly like he knows more than he wants to know, like he's woken from some long unnatural slumber to discover his inno-cence gone, leached from him while he slept. So that what he feels he's been denied is the slow truth about life – its drip-feed, its natural accrual of disappointments. In place of an insidious, systematic depletion of his faith in things, he feels plummeted painfully into consciousness.

Jean sees him smoking on the porch, his fleece pullover a slash of red against the white railing and floorboards and the dripping grey-green beyond the rail.

'All this inactivity,' she says, 'I don't think it's good for you.'

She worries, he knows, that he wallows in regret. Or that he's trying to remember things he's done. Or that he's thinking of a drink.

'Doing nothing can be dangerous,' she says.

'I just want to feel myself being here,' he says, and feels her look at him with pity.

Here. He takes a comfort in it he'd never have foreseen. He'd arrived on Jean's doorstep with a macabre sort of satisfaction, the sensation of having completed some unfortunately necessary mission. The act, perhaps, of having carried his own ashes to the sea.

On the bus ride north from California, he'd several times taken her address from his back pocket and checked it. To be sure he'd neither lost nor imagined it. Because the only thing keeping him going during that interminable journey was the pretence that someone was waiting for him at the other end. He was managing, too, at least until that stop they'd made in Medford, outside the hamburger place. He'd bought a vanilla milkshake and a packet of crackers that were a frightening radioactive orange and was sitting hunched on a bench with his snack, feeling the encroaching cold and reciting her address in his mind when he noticed it. The billboard. High up and straight in front of him, a huge picture of something gold glug-glugging into a glass and a pair of hands that managed somehow to look celebratory. And he had read:

You are here for a good time, not a long time

And then he'd noticed the bar, that bar with its open door, its darkness making a feeble attempt to spill forth but dissipating quickly in the daylight, as if whatever lived in there would die out here. A dribble of music was just audible, bloopy notes that moved magically skyward, ascending the bright air as though by stairs and momentarily bewitching him.

He had known every nook of that bar, without ever having been inside it. He'd known how it would feel to be in there, looking out. The deep comfort of being exactly where he needed to be, in the cool, mid-morning, dilating darkness, with something iced in front of him and, flanking him either side of the long bar, faces he knew without ever having seen them. The subtle gradations of anxiety, its varying manifestations. The averted eyes, the occasional cackle with no apparent cause, the mute exchanges, the bizarre fellowship of dread. And then each of them returning to himself, one by one, as though to sea level, having got there like having passed through the bends.

He'd shivered and hurried back to where the bus was idling and, reclaiming his seat, wrapped himself in his own arms.

He still wonders how he knocked on her door. Her house – with its stone-faced hush and Victorian uprightness, its intimidating symmetry – should have put him off. But when he'd found her address in that room in Sacramento, tossed among his few things, he had been visited by feelings of familiarity and shelter. He didn't know who had given him the address, or under what circumstances, but he knew he felt safer when he looked at it.

It was one of the many mysteries he used to run up against – of how something, somehow, could have registered in his mind, but in such a way as to have rendered itself irretrievable. He had often felt (and was almost invariably confirmed in his feeling) either well- or ill-disposed towards a person without having any idea why, only to learn later that the person had in fact done him either a good or a bad turn. Henry lived like a dreamer who had woken disturbed, unable to recall a single detail of the dream but absolutely certain of its spirit. He operated on the basis of a different form of memory than others did, one so deep that even blackout, with its otherwise scorched-earth thoroughness, couldn't touch.

In the end, it had hardly troubled him, this anomaly. If anything, he was comforted by it, for it enabled him to pretend that everything he forgot while drunk was in fact irrelevant, that memory itself – with its tedious slog of detail and discrepancy – might be perhaps beneath him. His life, as a result of these gaps, had come to resemble a series of disconnected scenes in which he, unwittingly, had played the lead. He had grown so used to being told what he'd done or where he'd been that even in the end – when there was no one left to tell him – he had continued to feel the presence of such 'informants'. He'd internalized the chorus, thereby creating his own brand of dramatic irony: he was both knowing audience and blissfully ignorant protagonist.

He'd felt posthumous, standing on her doorstep, steam rising off his wet pullover. She was his endpoint, somehow he knew that; there was nothing beyond her. They'd stared at each other in mutual bewilderment. They were somewhere that was once in a lifetime, beyond detail or explanation or appearance. Either she would help him or she wouldn't. Henry didn't have the resources to persuade her of anything except his need.

'A friend of mine gave me your address,' he said. 'In California.'

'I see,' she said. 'And who would that be?'

'His name is ...'

Actually, he wasn't even considering trying to lie to her.

'I don't remember,' he said.

She pursed her lips. 'Well, then,' she said, 'how about we start with your name?'

Jean is at work now, she works in the Maritime Museum and in
the evenings tells him stories of shipwrecks, booty washing into
shore, of Captain Cook dining on human arms, of all those lethal
failed attempts to get to the Columbia from the Pacific. She tells
him about her husband, who was a fisherman and had survived
numerous trips out but had died in a suburban swimming pool
after too much champagne.

'He wasn't even a drinker,' she says. 'Crazy, huh?'

In exchange, Henry tells her about his family and all the jobs
he's had and about how there's so much he can't remember. She
listens with her head to one side, drinking tea and smoking long
menthols. Night after night after night.

Henry has just hung the Christmas lights. He doesn't have a
job yet, but Jean gives him things to do around the house. Clean
the gutters, regrout the shower tiles, fix the garage door. Come
January, he'll have to get work. She knows someone who's reno-
vating houses and he can sand and varnish floors. For now, though,
he does what she asks him to and this morning it was hanging
lights. He'd had the television on while he was doing it, half-lis-
tening to the news, and was just hooking the last of the lights over
the front door when he heard it. One sound suddenly isolating
itself from the low TV hubbub, catching his attention, the way
the sound of his own name spoken in a crowd would. It was the
sound of Christmas Clydesdales, clomping, and that sweet homey
jingle: *daht-da-daht-da-daht-da-daht-da-daht-daht-daht.*

He pushed open the door, following the sound until he was
standing in front of the television staring intently at the scene – the
snow, the squat white horses, the familiar and oddly androgynous
voice-over – and was filled with an almost unbearable nostalgia, as
though it were an old home movie he'd happened on, of Christ-
mases past. The glow of neon in windows, the warmth of fire-

sides, acts of seasonal generosity. Hot toddies and egg-nog and mulled wine.

How many years ago was it? Nine? Ten? A Saturday morning in Virginia, Christmastime, and he was alone. The lights stretched baggily across the narrow streets and the air was tight with frost and he needed something, badly.

Through the muffled interior dusk of that bar a wide shaft of late morning light levitated. There were no other customers, but a cigarette smouldered unattended on the counter, sending little tumbleweeds of smoke wheeling soundlessly past him. Three or four small piles of sweepings lay on the floor, and he could hear the sound of someone shuffling about in the storeroom or the kitchen. He began to twitch slightly, his neck, his hand, his shoulder, one after the other, jumping. Had he a choice, he would have turned and walked out again. But he had no choice. He had a ruthless hangover, though *hangover* was a word he'd long since stopped applying to his own condition. For years, in fact, he'd hated the word. So uncomplicated, so entry-level, so charming even. People sporting sheepish hangovers were actually endearing. A hangover ... oh how he would've loved to have a hangover!

'How's it going, Henry.'

He cleared his throat, almost surprised to find himself visible, and said, 'Pull me a Bud, Frank.' His own voice sounding twangy and external to him, like a Jew's harp someone else was playing. And then, as though it were a mere afterthought and didn't much matter one way or another: 'Oh and a shot of something. A whiskey, I guess. And may as well make it a double.'

He listened to his own words drifting out over the air, seeming again to issue from a source other than himself. He felt involved in an act of simultaneous translation. He thought a garbled sentence, and then somewhere out there it was unscrambled, reprocessed, given wings, and handed over to be received and replied to.

'Okey-doke,' Frank said. 'What the man wants.'

He sat down in a shadowy corner booth to await his drinks. How friendly Frank had been that day, how obliging. What if he'd refused him? God, would he have had the fortitude to go through all that again in another bar? The walk there, the inside-outside shock, the unreality of his own voice? But he'd no reason to refuse him, not that Henry could think of (though there had been the woman that morning, yes, he needed to think about that). But no, Frank wouldn't refuse him, he was too kind, too incredibly kind. When he placed the drinks on Henry's table, Henry tried to smile at him in such a way as to let Frank know just how grateful he was, but the lower half of his face was still frozen from the cold, and anyway Frank didn't really look at him, just set the drinks down and turned away, whistling.

Henry watched himself reaching for the shot. Why had he ordered that beer? A cosmetic gesture maybe. It was civilized to be drinking beer at this hour of the morning. Perhaps he'd thought the beer would distract Frank from the fact that he had also ordered a double whiskey. So he had ordered the beer to 'impress' Frank. Wasn't that a little silly? Did he even care what Frank thought? Oh yes, very much, and no, not at all.

His hand, he noticed, had not yet reached the glass. OK, he was used to that, these split-second delays opening up in time and space, these lags between his thought and his action, so that he seemed to be watching himself under a strobe light. He struggled for control of his hand, his extremity, which felt so very independent of him, as removed from him as if it were one of those tiny toy cars, supposedly controlled by remote, but ever disobedient, operating with a mind of its own, stop-starting jerkily, now threatening to flip. He grasped his forearm tightly with his other hand and, lowering his head to meet the drink halfway, downed it.

He rested. 'Frank ...' *Fra-ahank*. He sounded whiny, like a boy whose voice hasn't broken. His head jerked towards the now-empty glass. Frank brought him another double and Henry drank it with slightly less trouble and then applied himself to the beer. One continuous swallow. Oh, it was wonderfully cool and refreshing, almost like having his mouth open under a waterfall. Like drinking from a cold mountain stream. Was that a jingle? Some ad he'd seen that was so accurate, it was masquerading as original thought? Ads had a neat way of doing that, of making him think they were his own thoughts.

Oh it had tasted good that beer. And he had needed something friendly like that. Besides the whiskey, which was necessary, and calming him already, he needed something gentler, too, something companionable like beer. He always felt a little innocent when drinking beer, like it hardly counted as drinking, like it was just a buddy tagging along, a kid he let play. And he needed that, because he felt sordid that morning. It wasn't just a hangover he had, even by his standards. He had woken up in that bed, next to that woman he'd never seen before, or obviously had seen, the previous night, but couldn't remember. He had woken, naked and on his belly, to the tickling sensation of her hand moving up the inside of his thigh. What was it she'd said?

You're like a cat, raising its rear.

She was bent over him, her hair brushing his ear, the tips of her breasts scuttling back and forth across his shoulder blades, her nipples multiplied and synchronized, like a little army of sand crabs scurrying across his back. Her fingertips were creeping higher up his thighs. She was trying to arouse him and he was afraid to even look at her. Never in his life, he thought, had he felt so naked.

When he'd managed, finally, to crick his neck and peek at her, the first thing he'd seen was a wedding ring. And then her face, plain, mid-forties, he guessed, no immediately visible abnormalities. He slowly turned over and lay on his back and searched her face. Nothing in it looked even vaguely familiar to him, but neither did anything look threatening, or injured, or angry.

He relaxed. Slightly. Those inventories that used to take him days – reassuring himself that the gaps in his memory were not large enough to accommodate any gross misdeeds – he could by then dispense with in minutes. But this was a new departure, waking in a stranger's bed (these little increments, booze nudging him always forward and he matching it, dare for dare, so that the two of them seemed engaged in a queer game of chicken). He'd have to file this one away, and file it quickly, but he was accustomed to that.

Then he thought he smelled sex in the room, and the little bit of comfort he'd felt evaporated. A flutter of dread passed through him and he knew suddenly that it was time to leave, not only this woman's room, but Virginia. Things had obviously gone wrong here, and he needed to leave, but first he needed a drink.

He'd made a rather abrupt exit, he really wasn't up to pretending he knew who she was or remembered what they'd done (this was not one of the amusing little puzzles drinking set him, like figuring out what day it was), and he certainly wasn't interested in anything remotely sexual. He'd been resting his left hand on his genitals underneath the sheets and they were soft as knotted socks.

She hadn't seemed overly distraught to see him go.

'Oh, if you must,' she said.

'Yes, I think I'd better.'

'Sure,' she said, 'but remember ...'

'Yes?'

'Our little secret,' she said, her finger to her lips.

God. He often thought blackouts were proof of a merciful one.

Sitting in his corner booth in the bar he felt both horrified and utterly unaffected, the way he might have watching footage on the six o'clock news of a catastrophic earthquake somewhere deep in the southern hemisphere.

About the previous night he felt alarmed but, bizarrely, a little proud as well. Of his tolerance for absurdity. Of his ability to face each day – no matter what madness had transpired last night – and dust himself off. He was practically smiling at the little picture he had in mind, of himself loping jauntily down the road after the treacherous start this morning had gotten off to. Look at him, he was here, he was fine, how many could say that after a morning like his, not to mention a night like last night, which he couldn't even remember. From this vantage point – of three doubles and a couple of beers and another of each on the way – other people's lives, rules, preoccupations, seemed suddenly infantile, naïve, pitiable even. It wasn't their fault that they felt at home in the world, content with it, resigned to its miserly drip-feed of sensation, any more than it was his fault that he wasn't.

It occurred to him then, and not for the first time, that they needed him, used him even, for he was out there doing what they dared not do: he was the one flapping perilously close to the sun, they were home watching it all on video. They were the cowards, and he, he was the hero. Yes, he thought, he was everybody's id. He did what they didn't dare, and then granted them the further favour of meekly, guiltily presenting himself for their condemnation, an object on which they could focus their disapproval, their pity, their terror. And all this they got without ever having to leave the safety of their own lives. What relief! What catharsis! He was practically a one-man tragedy. He should think about charging, for God's sake.

Time had grown continuous. His heart beat with a smug rhythm and his neck no longer twitched and he began to feel how good it was to be alive. He had seen right through the fuss of an hour ago, all that anxiety had been nothing but a chimera. He was visited by a great and ridiculous sense of accomplishment (as though it were he who had whipped the world and all its demons into shape), and he felt, there in his shadowy little corner, as though he were perched at some great height, observing the world with a monarchical detachment.

Really, it was as though his whole life were happening to someone else.

And yet of course not quite. For he remembered the need to be gone from here. He was not so detached that he could disregard his instincts of an hour ago. Seemingly unjustified fears had a funny way of turning out to be justified. Just because he couldn't remember was no reason to assume there was nothing *to* remember. Something occurred to him, a question, and he was suddenly, if briefly, bemused. Would he remember right now? he wondered. Or could you black out having remembered you'd had a blackout? Who was that woman, anyway? That married woman. And where was her husband? Who was her husband? Did he know him? And where had he met her? In here? Perhaps Frank knew her, perhaps he could think of a way to find out from Frank who she was, without letting Frank know that he himself didn't know. But that would be tricky, they would be verrrry tricky, that would require a balancing act he wasn't sure he was up to. And if he failed, if he let slip, well, it could get awkward. It was a small town and he was only a blow-in and Frank might've known her for years, might be a very close friend of hers, or worse, a close friend of her husband's. Perhaps Frank *was* her husband! Oh anything was possible. For all he knew, Frank could've been there! The three of them could've ...

'You OK over there?'

It was Frank. Friendly (but not too friendly) Frank. Strictly hetero Frank. Asking him if he was OK. Frank, whom he thought he'd been humouring. Oh no, it was the other way around, it was he – Henry – who was in the dark, who was being tolerated. How abruptly his mind could turn on him like that. How familiar the realization: that it was possible to be derisive and paranoid, if not at the same time, then by very quick turns. The line between hubris and self-loathing such a fine one.

'Perfect,' he called with a wave of his hand. 'Perfect, thanks.'

Jude had never seen a real German or, except for competitive swimmers, a man in a bikini swimsuit. Mr Bittner lived next door to them on Spring Street, where they'd moved the summer she turned thirteen. He owned his own small printing business and would often finish early on summer afternoons and work in the garden or sun himself in his navy blue bikini in his back yard while Jude, unbeknownst to him, would watch. It was her first live, up-close consideration of adult male genitalia, and Mr Bittner's, anyway, seemed pointier than she would've thought right, as though it were all elbows and knees. If you put a kitten in a sack, to drown it for instance, it would look like that, she thought, only not quite so stationary.

Revulsion and fascination battled for control of her mind. She felt about Mr Bittner's kitten a little like she felt about dissecting frogs in biology – perversely fascinated, revolted but riveted; she couldn't *not* look. But the more she looked, the more fascinated and less revolted she grew. It just became a thing she took for granted, a necessary object of study, maybe the way kids who are going to end up doctors just accept the fact of flayed frogs.

She accepted her interest in Mr Bittner's kitten, and in doing so felt some fate had been sealed.

Her mother befriended him. Mr Bittner had a wife who didn't come outdoors much. She was pale and blonde and dour and much more in keeping with how Jude thought Germans were supposed to be. But Mr Bittner and her mother would chat over the Bittners' sturdy waist-high fence, which bordered the quarter of their yard that their own bedraggled split-rail did not, swapping vegetables and recipes and newspapers.

'If you're going out back, would you give this to Mr Bittner, dear. It's yesterday's *Inquirer*. I promised I'd keep it for him.'

She stood at the fence, the *Inquirer* hanging forgotten from her hand. He lay with his eyes closed innocently to the sun. He was heavyset and very brown. A tangle of grey-black fur roamed across his chest. He reminded her of Marlon Brando, who was the first naked man she'd ever seen. (In later life, she realized what a lucky start she'd had.) He'd been right there on their coffee table, on the cover of *Time* magazine, in a lewd leg-lock with his French co-star. A still from a racy movie she was far too young to see.

Her eyes rested stupefied on Mr Bittner's groin. She felt as though his genitals were some recent and fantastic archaeological find to which she had privileged – but limited – access. A treasure discovered in a subterranean cave located on some other continent and she with only so much oxygen in her tank. She must attend to its details quickly and professionally, there'd be time enough for amazement when she surfaced.

Remembering her errand, she called to him. 'Um ... um ...'

'Aah.' He kicked his legs off the chaise longue. The kitten stirred in its sack. Her professionalism waned and she felt a wave of something like nausea that she had to admit was really neat and that she had by then learned to summon on cue by thinking of Mr Bittner doing things like kissing her. It was neat, he was like her toy. She could take him out and put him away whenever she wanted. At first she felt a little guilty about it, like she was somehow taking advantage of him, but she knew he could trust her. She would make him do nothing undignified. Indeed, he was gallant and generous and perpetually aflame. He kissed her perfectly, exactly as she was sure he would've wished to. And his vulnerability – his complete helplessness in the hands of her fantasy – only made him all the more attractive to her.

'Ah Jude, thank you,' he said, taking the paper. They stood inches apart, but with the prophylactic fence between them. 'Your mother was very good to remember.'

He didn't mispronounce many words – except her name, which came out sounding like *Zhude* – but his pronunciations were all exaggerated. As though each word were large and separate, and came booming from his mouth in bold-faced caps. He hadn't got the hang of contractions.

She could see the sweat glistening through the hair on his chest. His belly protruded just enough that, when standing face to face with him, she always felt as though he were pushing towards her.

'It is an old friend I knew in Germany,' he said, snapping open the paper. 'He has opened a German deli in Haddonfield. I believe there is a picture of him – oh yes! Look, there he is ...' He turned the paper for Jude to see. She leaned as far as she decently could over the fence. There was a photo of a curly-haired man with big black glasses standing behind a glass display case of cheese and sausages. There were Mr Bittner's square fleshy thumbs. There was his chest. And his belly. If she swung her eyes to the far right, they would be resting on his rough unshaven jaw, on his dark red lips so smooth against his flesh. Oh she was standing so close to him she could feel the actual heat off his skin. She had a sudden inspiration: she would ask him to tutor her in German! Yes, she'd always had a keen interest in speaking German and there just weren't enough opportunities! They could spend hours bent over a book, their head hairs even touching, oh but not in his house, nobody had ever been in his house, and certainly not in her house, with her mother and Bill schlepping around, no, they would have to go somewhere, somewhere quiet, somewhere private, they would have to go somewhere alone! She attempted to scan the article about his friend and inclined her head so that her exhaled breath would be directed at his bare chest. He pretended not to feel it.

'He quit his job of twenty-five years. He was a car manufacturer. Now he does what he wants. Finally.'

'That must be nice,' she said, trying her best to sound suggestive, though not so suggestive that she could not afterwards deny it, if necessary.

'Tell your mother I will bring her some strudel when I go next week. Dieter makes the best strudel.'

She smiled. 'OK.'

He made a baton of the paper and tapped her lightly on the head. 'How do you like your new house?'

'Oh it's fine,' she said cheerfully. Then, not wanting him to think she had never known anything better, said, 'I mean, it's alright. It's smaller than our last one.'

'A small place can be nice,' he said. 'Do you not think?'

She shrugged. 'It doesn't feel very nice.' Oh no. Now she sounded like a sourpuss. 'But maybe we just have to get used to it.'

'I am sure you have things to get used to, dear.' Dear? 'It will come, though. Do not worry. We adapt. We never think we are going to, but we always do. You will be fine. I am sure.'

Jude sighed. She felt suddenly heavy, as though she might cry. She wanted to be as sure of something, of anything, as Mr Bittner seemed to be of her ability to adapt. She looked at his roses, which were blooming at the border of his garden. She thought how nice it would be if he cut some for her. She thought about the word *adapt*, which sounded very like *adopt* but did not mean the same thing at all. It would be different if he'd said *adopt*. We adopt. What if he adopted her! Then she could live in his dark little house with him and see him as much as she wanted. They could sit around eating strudel and studying German all day long. She felt like putting her head on his chest and having him wrap his arms around her. She forgot about his kitten.

'Well ... anyway ...' She swung her eyes to the left and away from him.

'Do not forget to tell your mother about the strudel.'

He was always bringing stuff to her mother, mostly from his garden. Broad beans, heads of lettuce, tomatoes. He was so ... nurturing. Until they'd moved to Spring Street and met Mr Bittner, it had never occurred to Jude that men could garden and it certainly had never occurred to her that anyone who was not a farmer could grow food. Her father would mow the lawn and shear hedges and climb trees to lop off troublesome branches, but surely he would not have knelt before slender vines of tomatoes and gently, lovingly tied them to their stakes, as she had seen Mr Bittner do. Her father was more likely to have stepped on them, by accident.

'Why is their house always so dark,' she asked her mother. 'Why doesn't his wife ever come outside?'

'If I tell you, you have to promise not to say something silly or hurtful to Claus. OK?'

She would never hurt Mr Bittner. 'Of course not.'

60

'She's depressed.'

'Why?'

'There is no why. She just is. Some people just are.'

'But something must've happened. To make her depressed.' What had Mr Bittner done?

'Some people have a chemical imbalance in their brains, so that no matter what happens, they still feel bad. Mrs Bittner doesn't have enough happy chemicals –'

'Happy chemicals?' She wasn't five. 'You mean her serotonin levels are out of whack?' She'd remembered this from some anti-drugs literature she'd seen at school but she hardly thought she'd get the chance to use it so soon. Her mother looked worried.

'– so the doctors try and give her some,' she said, 'but it doesn't always help. And, she has migraines.'

'Ohhh, poor Mr Bittner!' Jude dropped onto the sofa. 'It must be terrible.'

Her mother looked at her. 'Mr Bittner's fine. It's Mrs Bittner that's suffering.'

'But he must be suffering too.'

'Well ... yes, I'm sure he is. But let's not forget, she can't even get out of bed some mornings.'

'It must be like a mosque in there,' Jude sighed.

'A mosque?'

'Yes,' she said, delighted at having got the chance not only to drop in something about serotonin, but also to slip in this clever new simile she'd learned.

'I think you mean a morgue,' her mother said.

'Oh.' Where had she heard that? On television. She'd thought they'd said a mosque. *Like a mosque in there.* 'Whatever.'

'Not whatever if you're in Egypt.'

'Well, I'm not in Egypt. I'm in New Jersey.'

'It doesn't matter if you're on Mars. You should know the difference between a mosque and a morgue.'

'I do!' Jude was losing patience. They were getting off the track. She wanted to know more about Mr Bittner, but she'd better cool it. Her sympathy seemed to be arousing her mother's suspicions.

'You do. Well, then don't be careless. And don't say to Claus that you are so sorry to hear his house is like a morgue. And for God's sake, don't say a mosque.'

In her fantasy, she relieved him from the darkness that was his lonely and heroic existence. He wore loose designer slacks, a short-sleeved dress shirt and a tie (never a bikini), and he was grateful beyond words. She was the one beacon of light in his life. He would come to her after some wretched day in the blackness of his home and she would comfort him. Innocently, at first, just being there for him as the grief that had amassed around his heart like some lethal fatty tissue began to melt away under her soft caresses and attentive ear. And he would drop to his knees in front of her, as though she were a tender tomato vine, and encircle her hips with his arms and press the side of his head to the fly of her cut-off Levi's and thank her for being so understanding, so wise beyond her years. She would stroke his greying thatch of hair. 'We adapt,' she'd say sagely. 'We don't think we ever will, but we do.'

'Ohhh, Jude ...' *Zhude. Zhude.* Her name on his foreign tongue.

And then she would manoeuvre him towards the short backless bench in the kitchen. With her fingertips on his shoulders, she would press him downwards, so that he was straddling the bench.

'Let me get you some iced tea, darling.'

He had come over to her house to ... to what? ... oh, to give her mother that copy of yesterday's *Inquirer* he'd promised to save. And here were some carrots, too! Only her mother and Bill had gone to ... oh they'd gone to New York for the day. New York? Yes, believe it or not, shopping in New York! So she'd invited Mr Bittner in because she could see he was terribly distressed, his life consisting of one dreary day after another, married to a woman who couldn't get out of bed in the morning. And then he'd wept, or nearly, in what would've been her lap, had she not been standing up. When she'd placed the glass of iced tea on the table beside him, they'd locked eyes and, well, they'd known. They'd just known.

He took her hand and placed it over his kitten and she squeezed it like it was that wrist flexor Bill used to build up his grip, only she didn't squeeze it quite that hard. She felt she knew her way around it, she had paid it such meticulous attention. She was a master cartographer who had mapped difficult terrain without actually having seen it and, on seeing it, knew it by her map. Mr Bittner moaned – he'd never been touched like that before! – and with his thick German tongue French-kissed her. She sat on him like he was a horse and with her fingers kneaded his chest hair, which was going every which way like a cheap shag carpet. They decided he would come over every day at four.

'I have to have you,' were his parting words. 'Oh, you are so beautiful, I have to have you.'

She could only sigh.

'And I must have you,' she managed finally, in a near-swoon.

'Tomorrow.'

'Tomorrow.'

They touched their fingertips to each other's lips, to seal their secret, and then she closed the door, leaning back against it and giving a quick shudder, as she had once seen someone in a movie do.

There are days he nearly wishes he could strip himself of history. Days he tells himself he'd be willing to forget the good parts too, if it meant he could forget the bad. Who would he be then, if he had no memory? If he woke one day and found himself an amnesiac, a complete amnesiac, would he still be a drunk? If he woke in a strange bed and didn't even know his name and was handed a snifter of brandy – a little pick-me-up – would he feel even the tiniest click of recognition?

Maybe, maybe not. Maybe, divested of his memories, he would suddenly be free. For his memories are all he has to go on, they are his only proof (there's no such thing as testing positive for his condition), they are the building blocks of his identity – they *are* his identity – so that he cannot think of himself without thinking of himself as a drunk. He is someone he knows by heart: he knew that he would drink, that he would get drunk, that he would be unable to stop himself. And he knew too that he'd forget. The irony isn't lost on him, that a 'condition' so marked by forgetting should appear to depend for its continuance on memory.

On the other hand, maybe it *is* him, his particular determinism, something that would always find him, no matter where he went or how much of himself he managed to lose. Maybe given enough time, the picture he now carries of himself would simply and inexorably re-form. Something like his breath on a window pane, visible and then dissolving, but always reappearing, and always his.

Now, it isn't a question of recalling things, of actively bringing them to mind, deciding that he will dwell on such and such a time. This isn't sentiment, or nostalgia, or even choice, it's not the gift of feeling memories washing bittersweetly over him. It's an assault: faces, lives, images streaming forth from his own depths. Now that he has paused, he feels often on the brink of an abyss, toeing the rim of a pit in which his past swirls.

Sometimes they come in silence, other times with an air of injured innocence, sometimes almost clamorous in their accusations, all vying at once for his attention. He has a sense of being under siege: as though to counter his sin of having fled, he has been reduced to this passivity, made subject to a pageant of apparitions.

His mother in the old kitchen, and he is sitting at the table, vacant-eyed, tracing with his finger the thin wisps of blue sealed under the laminate of Formica. He is eighteen and there is that old under-glass sensation, the airlessness of unvoiced grief and a morbid brand of piety. She stands with her back to him, pinning cloves into a side of ham. There is a large bowl of peeled potatoes on the counter, a dish of pineapple rings, a lemon cake. What is the occasion? A birthday maybe, or a visit from her sisters.

Beyond the plate-glass windows and the screened back door, everything is bathed in gold. The late-afternoon sun of early autumn. Soft gusts pull through the loose leaves; they flutter, settle, and flutter again. Soon, parallelograms of sunlight will stretch flat on the linoleum, as they have done day after day, year after year, a feature of his childhood, as fixed as the furniture that has never been rearranged. Over the years, he has played games in them, curling in the warm gold boxes as a child, a stowaway to some distant, always sunny place. Or danced in them, during his vaudeville phase, the kitchen floor a spotlit stage. And in his teens, when his father died and that rather macabre period followed, imagined them headstones listing in an overgrown graveyard, like those he saw when visiting his father's grave.

It was a heart attack, one spring evening while his father was coming home from the mines, when Henry was twelve. Two workmates had found him along the gravel path, his black tin lunch pail broken open in the dust. Henry sees it like a still from a film. Sees his father stopped suddenly in mid-stride, clawing at the air with one hand, clutching at his chest with the other. His mouth open, but no sound escaping; he can't even cry for help. Henry sees the reel running in his father's mind: his wife, his son, the lopped-off curve of his own life. The silver thermos rolls meaningfully down the hill and bumps to a halt in the ditch. He dies as the sun sets, as life is re-entering the earth.

His father's thermos is on the shelf now, above his mother's head. His lunch pail too. In her bedside table his wedding ring, and in the closet his coat and boots. Pieces of his life tucked like punctuation into hers. They are the conversations they never have about him. For she doesn't like to talk about him. There is no such thing as *Remember when* ... No such thing as loving, wistful laughter. Rather she has composed herself in an attitude of remembrance, surrounding herself with this array of inspirational props. It is an attitude he finds oppressive. Nobody knew yet about the 'stages of grief', and even if they had there is little doubt that she, at least, would have scorned them in favour of this doleful inertia.

She was dead two weeks before Henry even knew it. He had written her a letter – taking pains, as he did, to present her with a picture of his life that was not exactly a lie, but rather a partial and dressed-up truth – and in answer had received a letter of condolence from her lawyer. That was three years ago, while he was living in Texas, and he still squirms to think that while he was writing her that letter, while he was half-lying to her about his life, she was already dead, already underground. He'd liked to think he was protecting her from pain by glossing the details of his life, he used to feel mildly noble doing it. She had once used the word 'pitiful' to describe him, and he afterwards decided he would never provide her with cause to repeat the claim. His letters had become ridiculously chirpy. Who was he kidding? Not her, he thinks. But maybe deceiving her hadn't really been the point, maybe the point had been that there was someone left to deceive; that at least one person existed to whom it still mattered whether or not he was lying.

She died of a brain haemorrhage and for some time after her death Henry had been subject to horrific imaginings of blood gushing freely through her delicate head, drowning her. She'd been small-boned and very pale – he could even have described her as looking bloodless – and he could hardly believe her blood possessed a force or volume sufficient to kill her.

Now, when she comes to him, it is mostly with that familiar, slightly put-upon silence. Sometimes she is older – she was sixty-three the last time he saw her – and sometimes as brisk and fresh as in his very first recollections of her (though he cannot say if they are actual memories, or merely photographs so often seen they seem to him as animate as memories). He sees her standing open-armed, awash in that blonde late-afternoon light that used to fill her kitchen, a melancholic, beseeching look on her face, and he feels her struggling to awaken something in him: not so much the memory of her as of himself. He feels a downward pull, a dragging backward, a demand that he regress – impossibly – in order to relive his life.

His father sits quietly and off to one side, the image never placed in time, and yet somehow an image of time arrested. For that's how Henry feels him, sealed into the years before his death, unable to move either in time or in space. He is a large seated figure in his old black overcoat – one leg slung across the other, his arms folded atop his chest, his head crooked slightly sideways – observing Henry with a keen interest that recognizes, nonetheless, its own futility: he is dead, he knows, and cannot intercede on his son's behalf. He hovers vaguely like some ineffectual angel, but with none of the angel's omniscience. For his father is locked in unknowing, forever ignorant of who his son would become and reminding Henry, relentlessly, of his own once-blissful ignorance.

And then he sees his daughter. His daughter, who never drags him back but rather on and forward. Through all of her many selves, through the days they spent together, the inane banter, the complicity, the idle exchanges loaded with unspoken understanding. He feels pulled, as through a dream, or some underwater kingdom peopled with the most marvellous versions of themselves. Propelled by the sweet undulations of shared memory, they move in sync through this sea- or dream-scape, the surreal slow motion of love recalled. She leads him by the hand – as she had so many actual mornings – and he follows. And it is only here, with her, that he's granted the reprieve of participation.

They hurry clumsily through the soft dunes, slipping as they go, until all at once they see before them the beach, stretching emptily in both directions, sloping almost imperceptibly towards a flat sea that sparks under the morning sun. She designates a spot and they situate themselves among her scattered toys, and there build castles, fortresses, whole cities out of sand. Together filling buckets at the shoreline, lugging damp sand to their construction sight. She, so diligent beside him, insistent on carrying her own, a bucket hugged in both arms and her eyes assiduously on the ground: a single-mindedness that strikes him as a sort of dignity. Because whatever they build won't last. Even she foresees it. It will, by evening, be obliterated as thoroughly as if it had never been.

On all fours then, the two of them, the quick wrist-flips as they upturn their buckets atop the designated clearing. The scudding sound of fingernails on damp sand, hollowing a perimeter of moats. Her eyes on his hands as he sculpts turrets. And later perhaps, when her energy wanes, the listless building of what she's so dismissively coined 'instant' castles: handfuls of wet sand dribbled from their squeezed palms to form a confection of cones, an eerie cartoon netherworld, a city of stalagmites.

He used to hear her singing to herself, behind the curtain of hair that hid her face, as they laboured side by side, she lost in concentration and emitting – for they seemed rather to slip from her than to be sung – refrains from her little repertoire of tunes. (*On the Way to Cape May*, *You Are My Sunshine*, and, strangely, *Cumbayah*.) Listening to her, knowing she was unaware of his listening and even perhaps of her own singing, he felt, without the slightest trace of shame, admitted to her innocence.

And this is how he prefers to imagine her return: as with an offering of innocence, his life on a platter, given back to him.

The scenes she enacts for him excerpted from their best days together, the days of perfect, unarticulated sympathy. Days he was struck dumb with admiration for her. His fabulist, his little

diva, his playground revolutionary. The time he watched her
stage a walkout in their own backyard, taking all her playmates
with her and leaving her brother in an impotent rage. Bill was
nine the summer he'd drawn up that time-share scheme for the
play area in their back yard. Who could play with whom and for
how long: A gets along with B but not C, C gets along with D but
only if B is not present, and so on. He was like an actuary demys-
tifying existence. Henry had stood at the kitchen window –
drinking a beer and watching Bill with his clipboard and whistle
marshalling the other children on and off stage – thinking that in
nine years no act of his son's had so disheartened him.

Jude was following his orders, shuffling glumly on and off the
grass at prescribed intervals. But Henry could see from the way
she stood petulantly on the sidelines – her arms crossed over her
chest, her eyes following Bill wherever he walked – that discontent was brewing. And among the others, there seemed to be a
mounting confusion as to what to do when their turns came;
unused to 'playing' in such a contrived fashion, burdened by
repressed spontaneity, they had grown oddly self-conscious and
begun shoving one another around, while Bill looked on with
obvious displeasure.

And then she erupted. In a flurry of gestures and shouting –
and with one final exclamatory foot-stomp – she stormed off
stage, leaving the others looking somewhat relieved (if still
unsure of what to do) and her brother standing vanquished in her
sudden and impressive absence. Inwardly, Henry cheered.

She came striding into the house and when she saw him burst
into tears.

He sat her on his lap and she pushed her head into the crook
of his neck. With a purposeful absentmindedness she began to
pet his sideburns.

'What happened?' he asked.

'I like it better,' Jude snuffled, 'when you can play how you want. That's how it's supposed to be.'

'How what's supposed to be?'

'Play-*ying*,' she said.

'Well,' he said after a thoughtful pause, 'congratulations.'

She looked at him.

'You have just overthrown your first dictatorship.'

Soon after that, she entered the first of a number of phases in which she claimed to be transcending reality. At eleven, she was a stick figure scissor-kicking her way around the house. Wearing a pair of his pyjamas belted by a scarf of Mo's, she practised a brand of Confucianism popularized by prime-time TV. Affecting a white-knuckled serenity and insisting they all address her as Fierce Butterfly.

'Fierce Butterfly? But how can that be?'

'I am a fusion of opposites,' she said solemnly.

'My,' he said, and, gallantly playing along, asked how she had attained this wisdom, and at such a tender age.

She stood before him, looking mildly, endearingly pathetic in his huge pyjamas. Pushing her hair back from her face with one drooping sleeve, she said impatiently, 'I learned it on TV.'

Once, in her Confucian phase, she requested an increase in her allowance.

'But Fierce Butterfly,' he said, 'more money would only inhibit your spiritual growth.'

'Oh no,' she said, formally, graciously, gravely, her hands clasped loosely in front of her, 'I am sure that only by having money can I learn the un-value of it.'

'In your request is your blindness apparent.'

'... what?'

'Greed wears many masks, my little insect. And if I am your master, I must help you to see through your illusions –'

'You're not my master.'

'And on that illusion do your many others rest.'

'Hiiiiii ... yap!' She karate-chopped the mahogany coffee table, then turned on her heel and flicked her left leg out, switchblade-like, towards his belly – the signature kick she'd for months been perfecting in her bedroom.

By the following summer, all those flailing arms and legs had grown slack, her body rendered temporarily inert under the list-less influence of impending adolescence. She appeared as though under mild sedation, draping herself across the living-room sofa in a half-swoon.

'You're like a southern belle in a heat wave, dear,' her mother said.

She had discovered miniskirts, and begun teasing her long lank hair into a disaffected rage. She wore her mother's purple aviator sunglasses to the dinner table and, with one arm hooked over the chair back and her eyes focussed on some point on the ceiling, would endure dinner. Her free time was spent flopped on her bed under a Jimi Hendrix poster, the little pink plastic record player screaming, chocolate ice-cream turning to soup on her nightstand. No longer the Fierce Butterfly in search of enlight-enment, she was now The Shrug, a nickname Mo had given her, exasperated by her sullen stoicism.

And then she was off again, fired by a new idealism he assumed was the result of a recent television series on the Alcott family. She affected the bearing of a visionary and announced her intention of starting a commune.

'Prob'ly in Maine.'

'What are you going to call it?'

'Call it? Nothing. I mean I'm not going to call it anything. See ...' She sighed condescendingly. 'See, as soon as you name it something, people start putting it in a box. You know, like it should be this or that. And I want it to be, I want it to be able to be ... anything!'

'I see. I do see.'

'We'll grow all our own food and make our own furniture and nobody'll own anything.'

'Shrug's a communist,' Bill shrieked.

'I am not.'

'Commie!'

'Free love,' she said airily, ignoring him.

'Oh my,' Henry said.

'Oh gross,' Bill said.

'Do you even know what free love is?' Mo asked.

'Love', she said simply, 'that doesn't cost anything.'

Her father is standing in the hardware store, flipping a drill from his hip as though it were a six-shooter. Jude is four and squealing with delight. She does not yet understand that co-ownership of a hardware store is not exactly the romantic gallop through life he manages to make it appear. With only fairy tales as yet to draw on, she naturally believes that this dark, hirsute and huge-hearted giant can do anything he likes and has chosen to do this, and that this, therefore, must be the most wonderful life imaginable. She sees in his every exchange a confirmation of his power. He is asked a dizzying array of questions that, after all, he knows the answers to. He seems to her like an emperor granting life-saving favours with a reckless ease, a generous élan. He makes his customers so happy. Maybe they are happy because they know that something, however small, is about to get fixed. That life, after all, has its manageable moments.

Now, twenty-one years later, she knows better.

She walks up and down the aisles, fingering brackets and hooks and rungs, wrenches, hinges, curved segments of pipe. Though these were the very things she used to see when he was there, nothing else about the place itself has remained the same. The glassed-in office you had to step up and into, perfect picture of small-town self-importance, has been levelled. The old floorboards, which once looked bullet-ridden, are now sanded smooth and shining. The walls are festooned with big bright posters depicting smiling women on all fours, hammering nails or running petite hand-held sanders across their own sun-drenched floorboards. Gone is the large standing ashtray that had teetered beside the counter, precarious on its one stork-like leg. Her father's cigarettes had smouldered there, half-forgotten, smoke rising off them in a long, unbroken sulk, along with Jed's cigar butts which, split and stumpy, had looked like messily severed limbs strewn around a battlefield. Gone also is the sense of simple nut-and-bolt transaction, the air of being in a male domain. Jude overhears complex discussions on solar panelling, distressed furnishings, customers speaking to staff as though they were herbalists, or therapists.

Jed has long since retired and no one, of course, recognizes her. But she'd expected recognition to come from the place itself. That some evidence would exist, visible only to her. A trace of him against the far wall, where he was prone to lean. A blunt, almost ape-like outline of her father's shape, like the white lines drawn on pavements where murder victims have lain. But there is nothing.

Something, though, looks uncannily familiar, the rows of nails, loose in their big tilted boxes like sweets in an old drugstore. She likes that. That you can buy seven of a thing, or three, that a nail is still the basic unit of currency. She likes too the way everything seems to exist in relationships of reciprocal need, each thing with its corresponding counterpart: nuts and bolts, screws and screwdrivers, drills and bits, a hammer and a nail. She imagines how her father might have liked that too, the neatness of it. She imagines how he might have enjoyed being there, even when he hated it. How he might have found consoling the complete absence of anything abstract, the simple sense every single item made. She stands there trying to see the place as he had seen it, first as a kind of home, or a stomping ground at least, each nook intimately known and the inevitable comfort that must have come from that. Then as somewhere he couldn't bear to be anymore, part of a life he felt imprisoned by.

From where she stands she can see out to the corner of Fourth Street, and imagines herself occupying a carefully chosen vantage point from which she might snap some telling detail of the crime. In a moment of self-parody, she pictures herself a ham detective, a dick, working out of some fleabag motel just off 'the strip', this low-rent aura that can't conceal the big lumbering heart that beats beneath her regulation trench coat. She'd deliver the goods, she thought, whatever it took, and with her sense of battered decency intact. She can't remember exactly when she'd started doing this: method acting, couching anything important in make-believe. And watching it all happen, as though from on high, the experience and the simultaneous detachment from experience, her own running commentary like a cinema voice-over.

Somewhere in the midst of her reverie, she realizes that one of the employees is watching her from behind the counter. She refocuses and finds herself staring once again at a sea of nails and, as though having found at last what she was looking for, feigns delight (mostly for her own amusement) and gingerly scoops out a handful of two-inch lengths and brings them to the counter. Having made her purchase, she heads towards the door, towards the bright cold February day, the little brown paper parcel clutched in her coat pocket. She's tempted to whistle, as she is sure he must have on occasion, though she cannot actually recall him having done so. Opening the door, she waits, though for a moment she is unaware of what she's waiting for. It is the bell-tinkle signalling her departure. She had forgotten how she used to love the sound, in fact she had forgotten that such a sound had even once existed, and in the conspicuous silence that envelops her she registers the presence of something she'd seen inside but failed to actually notice: electronic surveillance perched high in the corner of the store. A tiny TV screen on which she has watched herself being watched. She walks to her car, disheartened, and places the sack of nails tenderly on the seat beside her.

He is alone in Jean's house. It is perfectly silent, but silence, he knows, possesses a sound all its own. He imagines it's the sound of time itself, audible only when all other noise has receded. Each moment passing as rhythmically and as markedly as a tap-drip, reminding him that it had never stopped passing, even when the din was such that he couldn't hear its passage.

How much of it he's lost he can't begin to know. He has 'woken' to find himself forty-eight, and he feels now the accumulated horror of all those mornings he woke to that cold and unwarranted clarity that announced the end of a bender, to find people – as though they were players he'd left frozen on a stage – now reanimated by his waking. And yet they hadn't been frozen, that was the awful thing. Life had gone on, people worked, news had been made and forgotten, schedules adhered to, the market had risen or fallen, the days of the week had mercilessly turned.

But each day he doesn't drink, he imagines time decelerating. He likes to think he can feel it. Feel the particles of time stand out from one another, like the hundred legs of a centipede on his skin. He courts tedium, half-believing that by rendering himself motionless and silent he is inviting all those years – the years that feel devoid of him, the years that have wheeled chaotically away – to come back to him. Even when he is reading, he stops in mid-stream and registers his own presence, almost shamed to discover that for minutes on end he has lost all awareness of time's passing.

Jean brings him books from the library.

'Read about yourself,' she says, not unkindly.

And he does, sometimes comforted by what he finds, sometimes not.

He learns, for instance, that he did not forget the things he'd done while drunk, but that his brain had never stored them to begin with. Or else had stored them 'improperly', half-heartedly, so that on certain days details from the night before or God knows when had risen up at him unbidden, arbitrarily, without context, and just as suddenly sunk back into the murk. He is mesmerized by the image of his double life and horrified to think that no matter how diligently he applies himself to its retrieval, half of it can never be retrieved.

Likewise, he is appalled to see his failures demythologized: his soul-sickness mere cellular damage, his nameless fears a depletion of thiamine, the huge thump of his aching heart an ailing autonomic nervous system, the bruising of his flesh a drop in the production of prothrombin. He has found in certain books blueprints for his behaviour – his very progress across the map and through the years as good as scripted. His deepest drives little more than a drink-lust, a lewd desire to be alone with his affliction.

He'd spent his life in flight, at first out of what felt like exuberance, then out of the need to escape banal domestic discord, the simple absence of joy. Gone then were those romantic midnight outings to the sea, those grand gestures to himself in which, like some poor creature unsuited to life on land, he'd crept back

79

to his beginnings. (Regressing, maybe, but knowing at least where home lay.) In time, when he left the house or left work, he got only so far as the bar, and then would find himself back in the hardware store, sitting in the raised glass office at the back, drinking gin, looking out over a sea of grey. Hardware was so grey. How had he found himself in such a colourless world?

Gin. If champagne served to elevate him above whatever seemed small and trifling (and what didn't seem small and trifling when drinking champagne?), admitting him to a certain aristocracy of indifference, gin, gin on the other hand, indicated a man who was fetchingly jaded, detached again from trivial concerns but now from a kind of feeling-fatigue. An unfeeling that was clearly the result of an excess of emotion and perception, a fate to which only the truly sensitive were subject. He felt himself surrounded by an emotional hoi polloi who were, he knew, incapable of ever grasping his grief.

Henry had always been prone to stepping outside of himself (when he wept, he wept unselfconsciously only briefly, and then began to appraise his crying, like a director deciding whether or not to cast himself), but sitting in a hardware store, perched above his little monotone kingdom (pouring tonic over gin, popping ice from the tray, slicing lemons even – what attention to detail! what weary panache!), his store of contemplative disdain felt depleted and he looked to himself like nothing more than a pathetic parody of his fantasies. He'd have much preferred to spy himself sipping mint juleps in the bourbon belt, or posed languidly at an umbrellaed table on a bleached terrace, gazing disconsolately at the Mediterranean.

One of those nights in the hardware store he'd felt it, the beginning of the end. Not the end of his drinking, no, that went on for years, but the end of illusion. He knew that night (though he didn't know how, or why) what until then he'd only suspected: that untainted joy was all behind him. He knew by then what went into such ecstasy like he knew how poisons can produce a paradoxical beauty – pollution rendered radiant at sunset, or the brilliant neons of slick toxicity – and in so knowing was robbed of it.

Sometime during that night he'd fallen asleep. When he woke, he was on the floor, his head wedged between the file cabinet and the mini-fridge. Jed's face loomed hugely over him, the bristle holes in his jaw were magnified obscenely, the wet pinkish maw of his open mouth was working, working: he was saying something. It seemed that Henry had woken up in the middle of a discussion, though why Jed should be talking to him while he was asleep (and apparently talking for some time because an explanation seemed to be coming to an end) he couldn't figure. Perhaps Henry had been awake and his hearing faculties just hadn't kicked in, though clearly he had now located the volume knob –

'... in a few minutes.'

'What?'

'She'll be here.'

'Who?'

'Mo, I said. C'mon. Sit up.' He put his hand down for Henry to grab and began trying to heave him up. Henry felt like one of those wooden figures connected at the joints by balls-and-sockets.

'For God's sake, Henry. Help me out.'

'I'm trying.'

Together, they succeeded in raising him to his knees.

Jed sighed heavily. 'This isn't funny anymore.'

Funny? Funny? 'Funny?' Henry said.

'We'll talk tomorrow. Tomorrow,' he pointed at him, 'we'll talk.' He hitched his hands under Henry's arms and guided him into the desk chair. 'For now, just sit here, OK? Just stay here until she comes. Don't move.'

'OK.'

'Do *not* move, do not come out on the floor, do you hear me?'

Jed descended the stairs from the office and Henry sat obediently at the desk, watching the customers – customers! – my, what time was it? They looked so funny down there, so small and funny, in their reds and blues moving up and down the aisles, it was like a board game they had at home where ten cardboard basketball players controlled by five little levers on each side slid along ten little channels cut into the plastic court. It was a terribly tedious game now that he thought of it, moronic really, each person would need at least five hands to make it any fun. And they'd spent hours at that thing, were they dimwits? These customers, browsing, browsing, scratching their chins like a nail was the biggest investment they'd ever make, were more exciting than those little cardboard men. Henry looked around him to see if there wasn't a keyboard or control panel he might use to speed them up a little, make them bump into each other, thinking how awfully funny he was for thinking that.

Oh yes it was fun up here, he didn't mind this at all. The only thing that would make it more fun was a drink. Something with a little *zing*, on ice. Something to bridge the gap between now – when he was feeling fine – and later this morning, when this precarious hilarity would be on the wane. It was important to build these bridges, especially in the morning. He could sit here all day then, perfectly content, sipping and watching and thinking his funny thoughts. Whee! he swung round in the swivel chair to celebrate ...

It was a bad idea. He jammed his foot against the desk to stop himself and, gripping the arms of the chair very tightly, closed his eyes, pursed his lips, gritted his teeth, and waited for the dizziness to pass. Suddenly, he wanted out of there. Quickly. Why had he thought being cooped up all day in an airless office watching a procession of morons shopping would be a pleasant way to pass the time? Was he out of his mind? The fluorescent lights were already inducing in him a nausea that, though it resembled car sickness, was really a nausea peculiar to being trapped under fluorescent lights (which made him wonder just what the hell fluorescent lights were doing to us), and then he noticed that he had become aware of their narcotic industrial drone. It had been there all along of course, but for whatever reason he had suddenly tuned in, and he knew from experience that at times like this once he had tuned into something unpleasant there was simply no way of tuning out.

But he couldn't leave. Jed had told him not to. *Told him not to?* Of course he could leave and he would, right now. But wait, no. Someone was coming for him. Mo. Mo was coming. Oh God. If he had one wish in all the world it was this: that she would drive him to the beach and that there would be no bad history between them. Just the two of them, a six-pack maybe or a bottle of something – nothing overboard, just enough to pass the day, enough to get drowsy on – and how about a picnic, yes, a basket full of fresh bread and his favourite salami, oranges and pretty purple plums. He could picture them – himself and Mo – lounging on the beach blanket (according to the calendar on the wall it was May, and there was no better time), they could play hearts and drink beer and maybe nap a little, they looked like kids from here, cosy as a couple of kids. Oh if he could just have one day – one single day – in which there was no remorse and no anger and nothing to make up for. Was it too much to ask? Just to help him over today, to be company for him, to have a drink with him and not be counting or calculating or worrying where it was all leading. Never mind what he deserved, wasn't life so short anyway? Wasn't it better they spend their time in forgiveness, in comforting one another rather than in condemnation? Was it really such a big deal, what he asked? Was any of it really such a big deal?

It was impossible, he knew, that such a day would ever come with her again, let alone this day. She would take him home and they would fight and he would have to figure a way to get out again. She would arrive and – and wasn't that her now? Yes, she was talking to Jed and they were looking at him. And then she nodded her head and then the two of them laughed – laughed! – not happily, not cruelly, but quietly and sadly, the way they might have if recalling the crazy antics of a recently deceased friend. He found himself feeling sad along with them, in fact unbearably sad, and as he sat watching them walking slowly towards him he realized with quiet surprise that for the last several minutes he'd forgotten to hear the fluorescent lights.

There seemed to be some question as to whether or not he could walk. Mo and Jed stood in the doorway of the office discussing who would take hold of which part of Henry's body while Henry sat politely and with commendable patience, as though perhaps they were customers having a hard time choosing between garden hoses and he rather magnanimously conveying by his expression: *Take all the time you need.* He did notice, however, that their faces had begun to throb in a way that he was not wholly unfamiliar with, but which no matter how many times he had seen it – or imagined he'd seen it – always threatened to derail him. It was as though something in them had been 'turned up', so that their physical beings seemed suddenly incapable of containing them. He knew from experience that when he landed on this particular square (for his mind swings seemed often as arbitrary as that, as moves decreed by dice rolls in some senseless board game) the sight of other human beings was simply too much for him. They stood there distending and deflating, a weird near-belligerence to their bodies, their faces, unnerving in the way that animation was. He looked at the floor, which was white and uncomplicated. Oh they had decided to lift him from the chair. That seemed silly. He felt wide awake, unpleasantly alert in fact, not the least bit noodly. But by God they were right, when he tried to stand he had that same ball-and-socket sensation in the knees and he buckled even as they held him.

'We can go out the side door,' he heard Jed say.

When they reached the car, Jed folded him into the back seat, squeezed Mo on the shoulder and then stepped up onto the sidewalk and watched them drive away, waving rather pitifully before turning back into the shop. Jed looked sad again, so sad, Henry thought his heart would break because he could see that Jed's heart was breaking, and breaking because of him. When Mo pulled away, Henry turned in his seat and through the back window watched the whole free world recede. If I ever go to jail, he thought, this is what it will feel like.

Jude is driving through Ohio, heading west on 70. Ahead of her, the highway's parallel lines converge in a neat geometric illusion, penciling towards the low, bloated sun. She pulls onto an exit ramp as the sun is all but disappearing behind a low cloudbank, an anaemic light spreading in the sky. A mid-sized town in the middle of Ohio, big enough for a couple of motels. Nothing is over two storeys high. Most of the offices are 'shingled' in what looks like wood but isn't and the motel itself appears to be made of plastic. (She gets a funny warm feeling and wonders how it is that a place so synthetic-looking could suggest to her a hokey, homespun decency. Shouldn't it be log cabins, or at least ersatz log cabins?) An elongated neon triangle is perched atop the roof. *Starr's*, it proclaims, with frantic cheer, in letters that decrease in size. The pink Vacancy sign is illuminated and the parking lot practically deserted. She feels an inverse thrill at having arrived at the middle of nowhere.

'Why not fly,' her mother had said, 'if you have to go. It's so much safer.'

'That', she said, 'would defeat the purpose.'

'Oh? Perhaps I'm not quite clear on the purpose, then.'

'I want to see something.'

'I thought you wanted to see him.'

'Oh ... you know what I mean.'

'That's the overstatement of the year.'

She checks in, and while the man behind the counter is running her credit card through a neat little machine that looks too much like a toy to contain information as momentous as whether or not she is a criminal, she notices the breakfast trolley.

'You can help yourself in the morning,' he says, gesturing towards the trolley. 'In fact you can help yourself now if you want.'

She looks at the trolley. There is a coffee dispenser (one of those tall cylindrical affairs that burp and sputter liquid when you push with superhuman strength on the large button), a tower of Styrofoam cups, and an array of individually cellophaned danishes, all of which look sat-on by people of varying weights. Another cup holds used stirring-sticks, and there is a trail of brown dribbles across the white tablecloth, which is not a tablecloth at all but rather a stiff, shiny piece of paper, something like a large disposable place-mat. She smiles at him.

'Thank you very much,' she says, feeling the strange desire to protect him from the knowledge that the world is full of places so much nicer than this one.

In her room, she flops on the bed and fans her arms over the spread, which is patterned in brown flowers. Brown? Tiredly, she wonders if brown flowers actually exist, and then notices that her entire room is done up in shades of brown. It doesn't show the dirt, of course, and she wonders just how much dirt is lurking unseen in all this brown. She thinks of an infrared light revealing layers of sloughed human debris – skin, hair, saliva. She feels a

87

dreadful fascination, a little like she'd felt when her cat had ring-worm and the fungus glowed a sudden neon green under the vet's magic light. She gets up off the bed. Her bathroom, she notices, has no windows, a set-up she has always found unnerving. One plastic sunflower rises stiffly from a vase on the shelf above the sink. There is a tamper-proof paper strip wound around the toilet seat, and clean towels, worn thin, are shingled along the plastic towel rod. She thinks again of the man in the lobby and feels inordinately sorry for him.

A television clicks on in the next room, and she can hear footsteps shuffling past her door. A tap running, a drawer closing, a cistern filling. She imagines the motel cross-sectioned: cells of privately enacted ritual, the low murmur of several simultaneous and unrelated lives. She'd discovered years ago that it's a fine line between what's pitiful and what's sweet. She learned it in the little house on Spring Street, where they'd moved after Henry'd left, the house that couldn't have been less spring-like. It had a strange quality of indoor shade – cool dank pockets, low ceilings, corners hunkering in shadow; even the furniture seemed to crouch. From the outside, the house appeared partially capsized. There was a low-slung look about it, it seemed to sag in the middle, to be sinking slightly, like something built for a quick buck on swampy land. It spoke of the small mean task of making ends meet. She'd tried to view it as romantic, their little fall from grace, to imagine them refugees from a gilded and glorious past. But instead it just seemed pitiful.

On Lincoln Street, it had all been different. There they'd been safe enough to affect a kind of carelessness. The house hadn't been luxurious, or formally elegant, or even especially tidy, but it had spread itself, rambled, and been generous with what it had. There'd been a sense there of things spilling over – clean clothes from plastic laundry baskets, from glass cupboards a small collection of trophies and curling photographs and autographed game balls, from the pantry, stockpiles of canned goods, canisters of pure white flour, jumbo packages of sweet things.

Midmornings, sunlight fell in stripes through the louvred blinds. Afternoons it rounded the corner of the house, stealing through panes of ceiling-high glass – wide flat sheets that thinned and lengthened as the day wore on. She could walk into a room and find herself steeped in a sudden shaft of brilliance.

The large back yard unfurled from the house at a slight angle of descent and their property line came to an end where the land suddenly dropped off, a steeper slope where began a rocky path that led to nowhere in particular. The absence of that far tree-line allowed for a view of distant suburban hills, and lent an air of open-endedness to the property, a sense of visual prerogative which fostered the illusion that what they saw, they owned.

On the back patio of fanned brick, deck chairs, tables and urned flowers idled randomly, like a small group of strangers distractedly aware of one another and all witnessing the same event. And in the liquor cabinet in the living room, tall bottles shouldered one another in a similarly offhanded alliance, their loud clashing colours and varying degrees of depletion making her think of a big box of Crayolas: the neon green of crème de menthe, the bleached-brick amber of sweet sherry, Kahlua like treacle, urine-yellow Galliano, and the brilliant blue of curaçao. You could, she'd once imagined, get drunk in a dozen different colours.

She wanders over to the bed again and sits gingerly on its edge. She can picture Henry in a place like this. There's nothing wrong with it, she reminds herself, it isn't dirty or dangerous or a front for anything illegal, it's even kind of folksy. It's just not a place any of them ever thought they'd be.

The Beautiful Changes

She almost smiles when she thinks of it, the image she used to have of him, gleaned, most likely, from a movie she'd once seen starring someone like Tony Curtis – slumbering poolside, flanked by women in bikinis and high heels, a rather gauche rendition of the good life. But she's almost certain it hasn't been like that. When she sees him now he is roaming through a vast, impersonal landscape, lost.

She could sense in his letters a spiral downwards. Post office boxes and odd addresses. Too many Care ofs. Once, a cafe in Texas. Did he work there? A short-order cook, they'd joked. Coming up in the world, Bill had said, way to go, Dad. She'd pictured him in a sweat-stained undershirt, surrounded by grease and grown meanly gaunt. Then, for nearly a year, somewhere in New Mexico. Moving furniture, it seemed. Sometimes, no return address at all, just a city and a state in a faint circular postmark. Places like Cleveland, which made her think of tire-tracked snow on slushy winter streets, or Rapid City, where she imagined sheriffs with spurs on their heels. Sometimes she knew he was drunk – his handwriting crawled spidery across the page and he dwelt on obscure scenes from her childhood.

Remember how you used to parade around the house in your mother's robe and that long purple scarf, you said you were an Arab sheikh! You must've seen something on tv and saying everybody had to obey you and the robe was so big for you you tripped over it, that's when I taught you how to say chic and then you were a chic sheikh, you thought that was a scream and whenever I see those velour bathrobes in the department stores I think of you, do you remember it too?

She didn't remember it at all, and was faintly embarrassed that he should cling to her childhood like that, raking it over for a kick or else solace. It made her feel pawed.

Other times his letters were overly formal, full of a strange circumspection, as though he'd been stationed some place by the CIA and was not directly responsible for his whereabouts or at liberty to discuss his actions. Then the letters just petered out until for more than six months she heard nothing. Then Christmas. Oregon of all places. You couldn't get much farther away without leaving the country. She sees his movements in her mind, meandering all the way across the map, tiny trace-lines like the trail of a slug.

The winters are wild here, he wrote. *Wind, and you wouldn't believe the rain. But I think it's a nice place. I think it's going to be OK here. I think everything is going to be OK.*

The word 'nesting' had come to mind. She imagined him foraging for bits of things to make his bed. A life that was small and humble. She gathered he was doing some kind of manual labour, carpentry in a house somebody was restoring, though he didn't say much about work, only that it was peaceful and that there wasn't a lot of it.

The coast is craggy, he wrote, *but beautiful. Nothing like at home.*
Home?
He felt, he said, like he was at land's end.
Tell me about your life.
My life? she'd written. Her life. What could she tell him? When she went to put it down, it too seemed small. *I work in a bookstore*, she wrote. *It's pretty peaceful too. I live in an apartment with my cat. We still go to the shore in the summertime (not the cat) and last summer I went camping for the first time, up near the Poconos. I go to the movies, and at work I can read, if it's not too busy. I'm learning how to cook. Can you cook?*

How could she explain that over the years so many spaces had come to exist solely to confirm his absence from them? That distance itself no longer had meaning aside from its capacity to measure what separated him from her. That what she dwelt on and even dreamed of were sights she imagined peculiar to the road: covered bridges, two-horse towns and all-night gas stations, the white interstate signs, hitchhikers, mesas, Dust Bowl dereliction, fields of wheat waving in a somehow patriotic breeze. An odd mix of decay and romance she could only have acquired from watching too many road movies.

What she said instead was that she'd be there in April, though she couldn't say exactly when, or how long she could stay.

I don't know what I'd like to see, she wrote. *The Pacific, I guess. What else can we see? Is it still raining every day? It's freezing here, but by then the roads should be OK. And don't worry, I always drive carefully.*

And he had written back to say that was fine, just fine, but he hadn't said much else. As though by tacit agreement, they were treating it like a funny coincidence, their happening to be in the same remote corner of the country at the same time.

By the time Henry reached New Mexico, he had begun to experience himself in the plural. Walking down the street, or riding in the furniture delivery van, he felt himself – or his selves – cleaving from one another, one part of him disengaging and ascending to some vantage point where it would hover, watchfully, a not quite disinterested observer of the other part, which continued miraculously to act, guided it seemed by some mechanism other than his mind.

Sometimes it was a merely curious sensation, a harmless out-of-body experience, half of him on automatic pilot, and he would marvel at his capacity to pull it off, to plausibly participate. He was an actor mouthing his lines and apparently they were the right ones, because other people mouthed back and whole conversations were coherently carried on. But sometimes it was horrifying – the sense of disconnection, the sense of not inhabiting himself. At its worst, it was like looking at the world without him in it. He saw life, he saw others in continuous interaction, and then saw himself, standing ghostlike at the periphery of it all. He was caught in a contradiction: sometimes sure that people were staring at him and at the same time wondering what they could be staring at; for he didn't feel material enough to attract attention. He didn't feel sufficiently there.

He was living in a small furnished apartment in Santa Fe, delivering furniture. He was, as they say, managing, but his life had become almost entirely devoted to keeping himself from falling utterly apart. He sweated, profusely and out of the blue or all night long. He was prone, whether drunk or sober, to sudden spells of weeping. His nose bled capriciously, his sheets were soaked, he 'functioned' as though his insides had been liquefied in some modern kitchen convenience. He pictured himself oozing, leaking, seeping, dehydrating to death, until all that was left of him was desiccated flesh and brittle bones.

He decided to stop drinking.

For the first time in his life. Entirely and for good. Though not all at once.

He drew up a set of rules. On any given evening, for instance, he would not buy more than one six-pack of beer and one pint of hard liquor. (To begin with. Later, he would lower his rations.) Once in for the night, he would not go out again. Not even to the corner grocery store, because in the corner grocery store they sold beer and wine, and even if he succeeded in getting out of there without buying either, he was then that much closer to the bar. And he forbade himself to go to bars. Too many people, too many variables, too many ways of losing count. Momentum was a constant source of danger. So, he would only drink alone, and he'd been doing that for years anyway.

He would avoid wine and also the company of women, for reasons not unrelated. Wine was voluptuous; red wine, after all, had body. When drinking from a wine glass he cupped the underside of its bowl with a tenderness he found crushingly resonant, he ran his fingertips lightly over its lip or up and down its stem, he planted his parted fingers atop its base in a gesture of what felt like possessiveness. A shot glass he held a little like a baseball, a beer bottle by the scruff of the neck, but a wine glass! – a wine glass possessed a particular topography that induced in him sentiment, loneliness, even desire. And if he was going to control his drinking, he would have to avoid becoming amorous or overly lonely. He would have to render his life as predictable as possible.

Armed then with his rule book, he stretched out on the single bed after work, sipping at his rations. He read the paper or *Time* or *National Geographic* under a low-watt bulb that it never occurred to him to change. He watched the news, sensing keenly, in the hours before dinner or bedtime, how displaced those unfamiliar faces and place names left him feeling. From his position on the bed, he could see his entire apartment – its kitchenette, its closet of a bathroom, the living room that was also the bedroom. It was so small he felt he was continually bumping into himself as he moved between its 'rooms'. When he needed space, he stepped out onto the breezeway and stood, massaging in turn his aching shoulders, lower back and forearms. He was on the second floor and from where he stood could see beneath him the parking lot, and beyond that a dusky indistinct expanse punctuated by a scattering of lights. It was twenty years or more since he'd been west of the Mississippi, and he had never seen a desert, or a tumbleweed, or a cactus that wasn't in a planter, had never stood in a city from which snow-capped peaks were visible. And yet, in the midst of these vast, empty spaces, he felt confined. He blamed it on the absence of the sea, which he yearned for, increasingly. His beloved sea, whose only constant was change, implying an endlessness to possibilities that all this land and light and stillness never could.

During those first months of enforced order (the weeks he'd thought it would take to wean himself had stretched to months), he regarded himself with a tenderness he found almost touching. A doctor-patient relationship had grown up between the two halves of him – there was the one who made decisions and the one who suffered, or escaped suffering, as a consequence – and he looked on his life as though it were an injured limb on which he wisely avoided putting too much weight.

Somewhere along the line, though, most likely during the third or fourth month of his confinement, he had abandoned the idea of giving up entirely. Having succeeded in reining himself in – and my God, it had been almost laughably easy – he now failed to see the point in going any further. What was the point? To be living just the life he was living without any reward at all? If he thought things were a little grey and drab now, he could not imagine what they would look like without even his few nightly tipples. Total abstinence, he realized, had been an idea conceived in desperation. He hadn't thought it through. He'd imagined the moment of giving up – his moment of triumph – but he hadn't imagined all the millions of moments after that.

He eyed his rations assembled atop the fridge – five cans in a huddle, a pint of gin (its little square shoulders thrown delightedly back), a litre bottle of Schweppes standing sentry – and regarded them with renewed affection. How helpless they looked! How winsomely bashful! And how disloyal and devious he felt, as though they were troublesome pets he'd planned to put down to make his life a little easier. But his life would not be easier without them. Look at them, he could almost see them nodding in agreement. There they stood in their defenceless little way, no longer pets now, but children who've counted off in class ('all the ones over here ...'), and he could no more cast them off than he could his own limbs.

A funny idea began to niggle at him, until his whole existence amounted to a swinging to and fro above this single fulcrum. It was, of course, the fantasy of exceeding his rations. Exceeding them so excessively that he would find himself smashed. Just once and all alone. He wanted to cavort with that side of himself so long neglected, so cruelly cast out. He missed him, after all, and rather petulantly. And the truth was, he was bored.

Anyway, this wasn't heaven. It was just existing. The old vague trepidation had never left him. He trembled slightly, and at the least provocation his trembling could escalate into a full-scale shake and heart-thump. He felt strangely womanish, fluttery, insufficiently weighted. And during daylight hours, he could be subject to a dreadful sense of unreality. Riding shotgun in the van, going from one ranch house to another, staring out into more blank, uninhabited space than he had ever seen, he was repeatedly alarmed by what broke the space. Freakishly large mascots jutting without context into the huge blue sky: growling tigers and stony-faced braves; bosomy blonde Frauleins twenty feet high, proffering plates of steaming strudel; a big brown bear in a red and white checked apron, crooking a paw at him outside a pancake house. Anywhere there was prolonged emptiness, there were these ghastly attempts to fill it. Hyper-real violations of space that seemed put there for no purpose other than to upset his fragile equilibrium.

'Hey,' he heard from the driver's seat, 'what say we grab a beer after work?'

'What?'

'I said why don't we grab a beer after work?'

A beer after work? 'No,' Henry said quickly.

'C'mon, why not?'

'Because I can't,' Henry said. 'I mean I can't make it tonight.'

He could feel Matt looking at him.

'What?' Henry said again.

'You're an odd fish.'

An odd fish? Was he an odd fish?

'What do you do with yourself anyway?' Matt asked. 'I've known you for ... how many months? Four, five? And not once have you come out for a beer with me, in all the times I've asked you.'

Henry felt trapped. He began to sweat. He wished they'd get to where they were going, so they could start unloading. He liked that part, just going back and forth from the truck to the house, taking his mind off his mind. He wished he were alone. He would be happy if he could do this job all alone. Just carrying things from one place to another (it didn't even matter where, back and forth would be fine) and not having to speak to anyone, ever. Other people only made it worse, looking at him, asking him questions, thinking he was an odd fish.

What if he came clean? What if he said to Matt right now: *You know, I have this funny feeling that you're not here at all, and yet you must be here, because you couldn't be unnerving me like this if you weren't.* What if he just said to him: *Go easy on me, will you, I think I'm going crazy.*

Maybe everything would be fine then. Maybe he wouldn't feel so alone. Maybe it was the pretending that was killing him. Maybe – just maybe! – they could go for a beer right then and there. Wouldn't that be wonderful? To fuck all his silly rules and just be with someone. He could nearly weep thinking of it. Just like old times, slipping in for a beer in the middle of a sunny afternoon, letting himself go because nothing terrible was going to happen, because after all they were just a couple of average guys out for a beer. Oh how Henry wanted to be average. To be normal. To belong, be one of the gang, know the rules and be allowed to play. But just existing, it seemed, was a skill he'd completely lost the hang of.

On the other hand, things might get worse if he told the truth. Matt might pull over, look right at him, and say: *Now hold on here, what exactly are we talking about, hunh? I think we'd better just turn around right now. I think we'd better get you back to base ...*

Henry couldn't handle that. He would collapse. He grew sad, he grew suddenly, overwhelmingly sad. He wanted to cry and had to bite his lip to stop himself. What had happened to him, anyway? How had he got to this stage where he was no longer equal to the most ordinary acts? Speaking and listening and seeing. He looked at his hands. They were his, and they were hands, but he felt so utterly, indescribably estranged from them, as though they were connected to him only as a thought is connected, some fleeting thing which just happens to be there and could just as easily be gone. He knew his hands were real, and yet like so many things that were real they had assumed the quality of an hallucination. Everything was backwards now, so that instead of trying to reassure himself that something frightening wasn't really there, he had to convince himself that real things really were there.

'Hey.'

'Hunh?' Henry flinched.

'Are you OK?' He sounded genuinely concerned. Didn't he? Henry realized he'd been drumming his fingers rapidly on his thigh. He stopped. Matt was worried about him. Why did Henry feel so sad whenever he heard that particular concern in someone else's voice? What had Matt said? Was he OK, yes, he'd asked him if he was OK. Was he? No! He most certainly was not. He was anything but OK, and it suddenly occurred to him that he could just say that. He could be not OK, he could be sick, people were sick all the time and they took days off from work because of it, and if anyone was sick, it was he – Henry – right now.

'Not really,' he said. 'No, actually I'm not really feeling very well.'

He could hear his voice quavering. He could feel Matt peering at him and now, instead of trying to look fine, Henry attempted to look as wretched as he felt. What luck! His terrible unease was finally working for him, Matt could see that he was definitely not OK, and Henry knew what he was going to do, he was going to take the day off and he was going to –

'In fact,' he said, 'I think I'd better get out.'

Seated in a small bar whose name he didn't catch with a pint of beer in front of him, Henry felt deliriously happy. He was so happy he could hardly contain himself; he wriggled. A small but rather idiotic smile kept nudging up the corners of his mouth. Here it was eleven in the morning and he was having a drink and by God was he enjoying it! When had he last enjoyed a drink this much? He couldn't even remember. Certainly not once over these past several months had he enjoyed a drink like he was enjoying this drink. He downed the first pint quickly, so quickly, so ravenously, he imagined himself afterwards chewing right through the glass – chompchompchomp until it was all gone – and then ordering another. He chuckled away to himself and ordered another, breathing a huge, happy sigh of relief. Here he was in a bar with money in his wallet and hours stretching emptily ahead of him.

Then he thought of his room, his sad little room. He thought of the television (its dumb look of trust when off) and of his neatly made bed, its sheet cuffed over its blanket, military style, its single pillow. He thought of his meagre provisions huddled together atop the fridge (looking suddenly, from here, a little too like a shrine), and felt a twinge of disloyalty, a shamed, half-adulterous thrill.

He looked around him. There were three or four people at the bar. A pinball machine he hadn't noticed in the corner. High in another corner was a television, some talk show with the sound turned all the way down. Everybody at the bar was glued to it. The air seemed suddenly brown and heavy; nothing moved. It was time for a change of scene, he decided. He was good at that, at sensing the precise moment of stagnancy. It was practically an art form, an alcoholic art form, knowing when a place was about to close in on him.

He stepped out into the bright sunshine, donned his sunglasses and, slipping his hands casually into the pockets of his work pants, headed at a happy clip towards the Number 10 stop. He must have cut a rather jaunty figure. He imagined himself doing a little dance, a quick hopscotch, light-footing it down the sidewalk like Fred Astaire, maybe pulling a bouquet from behind his back and presenting it gallantly to some female passer-by, tipping his non-existent hat, blowing her a debonair – but oops! – there was the bus just passing him by.

He ran, most undebonairly, for two blocks and caught it. He stood atop the steps inside the bus, sweating and breathless, and with trembling hands managed (it was like threading a needle) to manoeuvre his coins into the little glass receptacle. The driver pulled abruptly out, pitching him down the aisle.

The bus groaned and belched and Henry stared out through the smeared, tinted window at life going obliviously on and experienced a sudden and severe sense of deflation. He'd done it, hadn't he? He'd eluded his pursuers (Matt, his boss, his job, and yes, too, the miserable inner bureaucrat who'd monitored his intake every night) and yet his freedom felt so lonely. He'd have been happy to look back and find a posse on his tail. Instead, he was like a kid in a round of hide-and-seek who'd discovered the ultimate hiding place, one so clever that the others had wearied of the search. So here he sat, in his cramped nook, the thrill of having eluded detection waning, the sound of footsteps having died away. Nobody was looking for him.

He tried to laugh, but couldn't. Not even unkindly, and at himself. When he was feeling really awful he used to laugh, because laughing put him at a distance from himself. What a rake he was! What a nut! He became his own dubious audience, shaking his head with affectionate chagrin. And hadn't the others always been heartened to see him rise above himself like that? To see last night's frightful lunatic reduced to harmless farce?

He needed a pick-me-up. Quick. It was only noon, for God's sake, he had the whole day ahead of him, he couldn't let himself go downhill yet. The three pints had made him nicely woozy, but the wooziness was wearing off, and in its place a guilty panic was zinging through him. He had broken his rules, and anything could happen now. Couldn't it? Well, not exactly. Going back to his apartment, for instance, was out of the question. And he wasn't going to a movie, or for a walk, or back to work. In fact, he was probably never going back to work. No, only one thing was going to happen. He was going to get drunk, that was what was going to happen. And then anything could happen.

He had pretended to be fooled, but he wasn't fooled. Where had he thought it was all leading anyway, his silly little bookkeeping? Ah, drying out. Hadn't that been the original plan? Hadn't there been something about saving his own life? Oh yes indeedy, he knew very well there had. He felt sad, suddenly sad, remembering his heroic, ill-fated attempt at – at what? Controlled drinking? He could almost laugh, thinking of his drinking as a kind of untamed beast, and of himself there with his hammer and nails, his neat stack of planks, hastily cobbling together some rickety enclosure designed to 'control his drinking'. Oh but it wasn't going to last, you could see that from day one, it would topple in the first weak breeze, leaving the freed beast to go marauding through the landscape while Henry stood sheepishly by, his pathetic little tools scattered redundantly around him.

There it was, the place he'd passed so many times and longed for. The Relief Pitcher. Funny name, wasn't it? A bit obvious. Why not just call it Dying for a Drink. He got off at the next stop and thought of all the good exercise he was getting walking the four blocks back.

He ordered a pitcher – what else? – from the woman behind the bar, then chose a booth in the corner and sat there waiting so stiffly that rigor mortis crossed his mind. He made an attempt to loosen up, shrugging his shoulders several times in a way that made him feel like Elvis. He stopped. The woman was coming. She set the beer down on his table and he thanked her with such awkward formality he sounded to himself like someone only just learning English.

'You ... are ... welcome,' she said, teasing him.

He pushed his money across the table and waited for her to leave before pouring his beer. He felt a tremble coming on. He trembled with excitement or trepidation or both and thought suddenly of years ago, when the tremor had begun to appear arbitrarily, when he'd been feeling perfectly steady and had gone to lift his spoon and suddenly discovered he'd no control of his hand. It was horribly feathery, a weightlessness he'd come to loathe. If he was alone when it happened he could become rather fascinated by it, the way his hand had a mind of its own, and he would take it out and raise it tremulously, thinking of a symphony conductor issuing very delicate up-up-up instructions. But if he was in public or in company it was harrowing, he had to sit on his hands – wedge them underneath his thighs – to still them. He'd nearly been convinced he was coming down with Parkinson's, or some other frightful affliction, one perhaps he'd never even heard of. I think I'm developing a strange disease, he could still hear himself thinking. Strange disease indeed.

Here she came again, with his change, and he felt calm enough to look at her this time. She wore a white T-shirt, on which there were gold sequins arranged in the shape of a lion. Her jeans were a little too tight for his liking – or rather for his liking of her – and just there above the right hip pocket was a little silver label that read 'Sassy'. Her skin was a weird shade of brown, from too much sun, and she wore blue eye make-up. Her hair was frosted blond and her fingernails painted an icy white. Every detail of her was in violent argument with every other detail and he wondered – in the way he sometimes did when he saw women who were totally alien to his preferences – if he could ever sleep with her. She was holding a long brown cigarette the colour of her face, a More, he guessed. *Amor*, he thought happily, then very sadly.

She pulled on her *amor* and said, 'Do you live here? I haven't seen you before.'

'Well, in a way I guess I do,' he drawled – he was drawling! he wasn't even a drawler – 'but it's really just a kind of ... phase.' A phase. A phase? What ever did he mean by that?

'A phase,' she said. 'Me too. I'm going through a phase too.'

'Yeah?'

'Yeah,' she said. 'It's called my life. Hah!' She walked away, laughing over her shoulder.

'Hah-hah!' he laughed along, though it was not a joke he found funny.

He sipped at his beer and pushed the plastic pitcher to and fro across the table. The relief pitcher. The relief pitcher! Oh he got it. It was a baseball pun. How had he missed that? Boy he really was getting dull. He smiled. Thinking of sunny days in the park long ago. Warm spring sun on his bare arms and for afterwards a cooler full of beer that didn't mean anything, didn't spell big trouble or the first step on the way to some new catastrophe. To distract himself from the past, he looked quickly towards the bar, just in time to see Sassy moving her balled brown fists in tight little circles in front of her chest, thrusting one shoulder forward, then the other. She was looking at a man in a white apron who had come through the swing doors behind the bar.

'Dancing tonight,' she called to Henry, when she saw him watching her. 'You like dancing?'

He smiled wanly and raised his glass. It wiggled slightly in mid-air and he quickly lowered it again.

'Owh! We've got a dancer over here, Mick. You'd know just by the look of him. Look at him, Mick.'

Mick looked at him and grunted.

It occurred to Henry that he should just go. It wasn't too late. He could get up and leave now. He wasn't having much fun, was he? Fun. Fun. Fun. He rolled the word over and over in his mind until it began to sound not like a real word at all. Fun. Funnn. Fuuun. This wasn't fun and he go could go somewhere else, he could do something else. He could stop drinking, for instance. Right here in this bar, in The Relief Pitcher. (He saw himself passing, years from now, and pointing it out to some sweet companion: *Right there*, he would say, *right there's where it happened, where I just up and called a halt. Zip. End of story. No more drink.* And she would gaze admiringly at him and link his arm and they would stroll contentedly away.) It could happen – these things did – this very beer could be the last drink he ever had. He looked at the near-empty pitcher on the table. He drew back from it and pursed his lips, tilted his head to one side and squinted at it, trying to see it as his Last Drink.

My. It looked oddly unimpressive. It seemed lacking in stature, a little too humble to be saddled with history-making. He eyed it regretfully. No, he was terribly sorry to have to say this, but it just wouldn't do. There was something definitely wrong with the idea of this beer – which he hadn't ordered thinking it would be his last drink – actually being his last. It was so accidental, it was sloppy, careless, haphazard, it was lacking in the appropriate ceremony. It didn't bode well, this doing things at the drop of a hat. Not this thing anyway. And a beer, for God's sake! What was he thinking? That after all this time, after his long trawl through the multifarious concoctions and combinations (the shaken and the stirred, the rainbow of liqueurs, the tri-colour of red-white-rosé), that he should end his days – his comic-tragic drinking life – with something as insipid and meaningless and entry-level as a lukewarm second-rate domestic beer. No! Every fibre of his being clamoured for panache. Make no mistake about it, he thought, there's a bit of style in the old boy yet!

Better he should order a double gin – a Tanqueray perhaps, or better yet two, two at once – and finish the thing right. His parting shot. (Parting shot, he didn't miss that one, did he?) Or how about a bottle of champagne? Perhaps, for his swan song, he should polish off a bottle of champagne ... but no, that would be striking the wrong note. Champagne marked the beginnings of things – boats and babies' lives and corporate mergers – but not sobriety. Gin, though, was strictly business, you sealed things over gin. Yes, that was what he would do, he would seal his impending sobriety over a double gin. Or rather two. He would order two double gins, with tonic and lime – Tanqueray and tonic, now there was a drink with a bit of poetry to it – and when he'd finished the second one, he would set his glass down authoritatively and he would get up and stride out of this dive, never to be seen again. And there they would stand, Sassy and Mick, in stupefied silence, reverent in the wake of his departure, thinking *Who was that man? Who was that decisive man?*

'Sassy,' he called, feeling suddenly chipper (a touch of the dandy about him, if he had a cane he'd swing it) now that he knew that within half an hour his life would never be the same again.

Sassy walked towards him with her neck craned as though to say *I'm not quite sure I heard you right, you jerkoff*, when of course she'd heard him perfectly and they both knew that. He pointed to her little silver label and she laughed.

'Oh, that,' she said.

He ordered a double gin. No point in ordering two at once, the ice would only melt. And besides, he didn't want to rush. He wanted to do the thing right.

'No Tanqueray,' she said. 'Gilbey's.'

'Gilbey's, hunh?' The first chink in his plan. This wasn't good. Why was it that just when he'd mapped his exit so beautifully Sassy had to throw a wrench into things? 'Well,' he said, 'Gilbey's it is then.' And as he watched her turn on her heel and sashay non-nonchalantly back to the bar, he experienced a kind of omniscience that smacked of criminality. For little did she know what was taking place under her very nose. Little did she know that she had just taken his order for the Second-To-Last-Drink he would ever have.

*

What happened?

Henry was lying on his back in his own bed and it was bright outside. The ceiling fan was whirring so fast he had to close his eyes. But closing his eyes somehow made the fan louder, as loud as chopper blades that had come loose from their moorings and were whirring, lethally, ever nearer to him. He opened his eyes again quickly and raised himself to a sitting position. He was heavy, he was fully clothed. He looked up at the ceiling fan and steeled himself for the task of pulling its cord. He got to his feet and stood wavering beneath it. He had to be careful, it was difficult to judge the distance and the cord was bouncing slightly in the breeze; he imagined his severed hand waving to him as it sailed across the room.

He reached up and tugged gingerly on the cord, and as he heard its dull click he remembered two women.

He got back into bed and then got out again. He decided to brush his teeth – that was good, that was never a bad idea, he could always be sure he was doing something right when he brushed his teeth. But he found the appalling taste in his mouth altered rather than removed; instead of a fungal clamminess, there was now that familiar morning-after feel of corrosive metals, of his whole mouth being made of rust. He noticed a strong smell of formaldehyde – or what he imagined formaldehyde would smell like – hanging over the room. A chemical tang that made him think of his insides pickling.

What had happened was, he'd met two women. In the middle of his second gin. When he was only half a drink away from the beginning of the rest of his life, he'd made the mistake of talking to two women. They were sitting at the next table and had been there as long as he had, though it was only when the bar began to fill a little that he started speaking to them. In the midst of a growing number of strangers, they'd been relatively less strange. A funny, unspoken affinity had risen up between the three of them, as though they were the longest-waiting passengers for a long-delayed flight.

They joined him at his table and on the way called for another pitcher.

'Be nice to him, girls,' Sassy called, 'he's going through a phase.'

Very companionably they'd poured him a beer from their pitcher, without even asking, without even checking if perhaps he hadn't been just about to stop drinking forever. He watched the beer rising foamily up the height of his glass and felt a deflation that was awash in relief.

He'd hesitated. For thirty seconds or so he allowed his selves to jabber back and forth, one of them pleading – however meekly – for a new life, the other growing increasingly derisive of those pleas.

They'd all laughed about it then, because he'd told them, hadn't he ...

'Do you know where I was headed just before I met you guys?' he'd said. 'Can you believe that?'

No, they couldn't believe it. And so he'd told them all about his life – his recent life, anyway – in the apartment, with his rations and his *National Geographic*, his oxymoronic controlled drinking (yes, he'd told them about that too), his idiotic job and his dim-witted partner. He'd drawn such a hilarious caricature of his life and oh how they'd laughed. They thought he was so funny, they thought he was cute, yes, he remembered that.

'You're cute,' one of them had said and the other had smiled.

They hadn't been flirting really, he was like a loveable little thing to them, a puppy, maybe, who was following them around a carnival. But then she'd also said, some time later and with a funny half-fearful, half-concerned look on her face, 'You'd wanna watch it, though, you know, you'd wanna be careful ...'

And he'd waved off her concerns with a big brave sweep of his hand.

Henry was sitting on the bed, moving his tongue around the rusty interior of his mouth. On the floor before him, shiny and new amidst yesterday's detritus, was what looked like a coffee-table book. Had he bought himself a coffee-table book? He, who didn't own a coffee table? He bent down, fished it out from under his socks, and opened it. It was full of beautiful glossy pictures of Native Americans. He turned the front cover over. *The Anasazi*, it said. His own voice came back to him. 'I know, of course,' it was saying, 'that Native Americans were here before us, I know they're real and they live here and they have lived here for, oh, forever, but I can't help feeling, I mean I'm ashamed to say it, but I can't help feeling –'

'Yeah?'

'Like when I see them I'm in a theme park.'

'Oooh.'

'Like when we turn our backs, they'll just troop offstage.' Oh God, had he said that? He had. 'But the thing is, the thing is, who's conning who? Who's conning whom? That sounds sick, doesn't it, and I don't mean it to be sick, I'm not sick –'

'Nah,' the blonde said, her hand resting consolingly on his arm, 'it's not sick.'

'It's not sick,' the less blonde agreed. 'It's just post-modern.'

'Post-modern? Do you think so?'

'Oh definitely. Hum-hum' – he never did catch her their names – 'hum-hum here is doing post-modern studies at U ...' U something.

'It's not post-modern studies –'

'Well, what?'

'It's *culture* studies.'

'Same thing.'

'Hardly.'

'Wait!' Henry said, 'I've got an idea!'

And that was when he'd suggested they all go to the Anasazi craft shop. He said they should learn something and not be just sitting around drinking all day – 'OK, *Daaad*' – and that was how he'd ended up with the coffee-table book.

He slowly turned the pages. Amazing. Little apartments hollowed into high cliffs. People living, literally, on the edge. He knew how they felt. 1100 AD, my God, and then suddenly, they'd just up and disappeared.

He wished he'd been an anthropologist. How different his life could have been, how exciting, how rewarding! He'd have loved that, digging around in the dirt all day, in the warm sun, finding fascinating remnants of other civilizations, publishing papers throwing astonishing new light on the history of mankind.

Instead, he was nothing. He was a furniture mover, and not even that anymore. He was an out-of-work dipso. One day he would die and then what? Nothing. In the whole huge scheme of things, in all the history of his species, all the making and doing and inventing and evolving, in every little act that spawned every other act so that people's lives from long ago looked like childish imitations of adult mannerisms and then ... oh! When photography came! That was something else, it was heart-rending, the way it captured those people always with that terrible seriousness of purpose in their eyes, as though they knew the whole future depended on them and were going to do their damnedest to be equal to the task.

The family of man, he thought. Not one little thing could they say he'd added to it. And now he was leaving again. He hadn't known it until that very moment, but once he'd thought it, he realized it was true. He would go. He would go to California, he would go to California and he would see the sea. He would smell it! He would swim in it too and he would feel OK again. He wished he were there right now. He couldn't stand one more minute in this place, this state, so far from the sea. He felt a little better now, now he knew that he was going. Leaving had always been the very best of all and that was one thing about him, he knew when it was time to go. He looked around him. At his clothes on the floor, at last week's newspapers, at dishes from yesterday's breakfast. How long ago it seemed! Yesterday. The book was still lying open on his lap and he looked at that. All that adobe and blue sky, the colours he could hardly bear to see, all the beautiful things in life, all the mysteries of man that he would never unravel. Everything reminding him of everything he wasn't.

'Bill?'

'Jude? Where are you?'

'Not far from Peoria.'

'Peoria where?'

'You don't know where Peoria is? My God. Americans and geography.'

'Illinois,' Bill says.

'Ah. See. You did know. Why do you pretend you don't know when you do? You're under-achieving again,' she says. 'If only you'd gone to that all-girls school, you'd be president by now.'

'Swim first, then be the president.'

'What?'

'This Asian woman in my office. She said when she was grow-ing up in California, she thought that was the American dream.'

'Why swim?'

'In her swimming lessons when she was a kid, there was this boy who was obsessed with being president when he grew up and he wouldn't get into the pool. So his mother said: Swim first, *then* be the president.'

'Hmm. How catchy. I'm sure Cuban refugees could identify.'

'Cuban refugees could never become president.'

'Oh yeah, of course. Well, anyway ...'

'How is it?'

'It's very ... corn-y. Apparently. Though I've only ever seen corn in a can, you know, floating in that yellow goo.'

'I meant the trip,' Bill says.

'Oh. OK. Bill ...?'

'Yeah?'

'Did you know that Chicago has the second-largest population of Poles in the world, after Warsaw?'

'You're kidding. And what's the bad news?'

'That for every Pole in Chicago, there is apparently a sports bar somewhere else in Illinois. They're killing me. I keep ending up in them by accident.'

'How can you end up in a sports bar by accident?'

'Well the doors are small and wooden and from the outside they look just like charming little Alpine taverns. And then you go in and it's this neon emporium with two-storey televisions on every wall.'

'Poor Jude. Deceived by appearances.'

'Yeah. Well. I've become kind of fatalistic about it. I'd be disappointed, I think, if I didn't end up in one tonight.'

'What a grim fascination.'

'Bill ...?'

'Yeah?'

'Remember when we were going to travel around the world on horseback?'

'Um, vaguely. When was it, exactly?'

'Oh, last year, I think.'

'Of course. Right before I grew up.'

'Yes, I tried to stop you, but you insisted.'

'I wouldn't mind.'

'Growing up?'

'Or travelling around on horseback.'

'Yeah? Well don't go till I get back.'

'Are you coming back?'

'Of course. What in the world would I do in Oregon?'

'What does anybody do in Oregon?'

'I'll let you know.'

'Are you sure you're OK?'

'Yeah. It just feels like I've been gone for years,' she says. 'Does it feel like that to you?'

'I feel ...'

'What?'

'Oh, I don't know.'

'A grim fascination?'

She doesn't find a sports bar. Illinois is like that, she thinks. It's so dumb you can't even be ironic in it. Instead she eats chicken burritos in a black and silver place, furnished in the kind of Scandinavian minimalism found in certain McDonalds. Swim first, then be the president. All over Peoria, she thinks, there are kids who believe they will one day be president. She gives a little hoorah for dumb dreams.

Two guys down the bar are eyeing her. She turns in her chair so that her back is to them. One of them looks a little like the phone jack, and thinking of him makes her sad. What was *that* about? He used to come into the bar where she was working last year and she'd imagine him thirty feet up, thighs clamped around some humming pole. Her urban lumberjack. He was big and burly and fortyish, recently separated. During one of their mind-less, fawning exchanges across the bar, she'd managed to find out exactly where he was working and the following day had driven slowly past, then parked down the street to watch. His rear strapped into some kind of harness, tools dangling from around his waist like a grass skirt made of metal implements. So cool and undaunted in his obvious imperilment, all so she could get a dial tone, order a take-away pizza if she felt like it. Her very own unsung hero, one of those silent forces that made her world go round, like the high-school janitor who used to invade her dreams. Bearded twenty-something with a sloppy swagger and a big ring of keys swinging masterful and nonchalant from his belt loop, wheeling the garbage trolley down the empty halls in the eerie after-school hush. She used to spy his silhouette approaching from afar and the two of them would stroll towards each other in the shadowy silence, all the dangerous drama of a surreptitious rendezvous. She'd never have spoken to him – it just wasn't done, fraternizing with janitors – but she used to drill her eyes into his as she passed.

The night after the day she'd watched the phone jack at work, she went home with him. Being in his apartment was like being inside a set of fibre-board cupboards. Even the sandwich he made her seemed synthetic.

'It came furnished,' he boasted. 'But the pictures are mine.'

Hot diggety dog, she thought, and nuzzled her knee into his groin. Things went swimmingly for nearly a month, all she had to do was think of him up the pole and the rest took care of itself, but finally he'd insisted on taking her out for a 'big dinner'. She'd have been happier under his polyester bedspread, losing herself in the fur and heft of him, pretending she was a moll in a cult seventies film and he a small-time drug dealer. Had he a violent streak? Oh, maybe. Anything was better than that goofy look in his eyes.

Dinner was a disaster. As soon as they sat down she knew it. In public, she couldn't bring herself to touch him; that charming air of vulnerable incomprehension that had so appealed to her seemed suddenly nothing more than dim-wittedness. He talked about going on vacation to Guadalajara together – he could teach her to bungee jump, or was it parasail? – and she nodded politely, knowing these were the last two hours she would ever spend with him. She'd never have been rude enough to rush through dinner, though, and remembering something her mother once had said – *you can learn something from everyone you meet* – had asked him to explain to her the guiding principle behind telephonic communication. Which he had, at length. Only instead of restoring him to his former glory, as she had hoped (if only for the duration of dinner), his expertise bored her and the pride he took in it irked her. She wanted to cry.

He couldn't understand why she wouldn't go home with him that night and how could she say that being with him made her unbearably lonely?

'I don't get it,' he said, looking bewildered.

And she knew he didn't. Standing beside their respective cars, which were parked side by side in the lot, she knew that he was wondering if it was over, and was waiting to be given some sign. She felt a little stab of tenderness and a fleeting temptation to forget all their differences and just be with him, as though that split-second of affection might be enough to go on. But of course it wasn't. It was all so pathetic, in the most endearing kind of way. She and the phone jack standing there in the dark, with not a single thing to say to each other, nothing but this shared, shamed admission of the fact that they had completely missed the point of each other and nothing – not all the split-seconds in the world – was ever going to change that.

It was Bill who had christened him the phone jack.

'What happened?' he asked. 'I thought it was such a ... good connection.'

'Oh, one of those nights,' she said vaguely.

'Dare I ask? One of what nights?'

She thought hard. 'I looked my life in the eye,' she said, 'and my life sort of averted its gaze.'

'Ohhh,' he said. 'Ouch.'

She leaves early the next morning and heads north towards 80. Downtowns that appear to consist wholly of Formica, plastic, and unlit neon. Used-car lots that stretch for blocks, those plastic triangular flags peculiar to the trade strung round their perimeters, flapping in the breeze with a tattered gaiety. It's the kind of landscape in which she has often imagined finding him. Her father standing on the roadside like a sad case, a harmless hobo straight out of the thirties, his swag on the end of a stick. A decent sort who through no fault of his own had gone astray, marooned now at some dusty crossroads, waiting to be recognized and rescued.

But really. He could be living in a trailer park for all she knows (despite his letters and the rainy domesticity they suggest, she won't believe until she sees), could be living with some ornery, bedraggled woman with bags under her eyes and a bare midriff screeching at him as she schleps around their kitchenette, while he slouches on the sofa in a sweaty undershirt and boxers, dirt-streaked urchins who claim to belong to him scurrying about his feet. Or worse, perhaps, he might be alone, living in an SRO, wet-brained and watching *Wheel of Fortune*. And she will have to sit there with him and over a plate of pork and beans remind him repeatedly of who she is.

Then what? Can she go home then? Go home and begin her new life as a 'sexually viable adult'? Yes, it was true, she had read it. Horrified, she had sat behind the counter at the book store and seen herself unmasked in black and white, a case study in a psychoanalytic textbook. It was so diminishing – diminishing? – it was devastating. Here she'd thought of herself as harmlessly kooky, lovably out of whack; she had a few manageable little quirks, and she regarded these with tender irony. She wasn't exactly happy about the little hiccups in her personal development, but they weren't serious, and anyway, at least they were hers, the hiccups. But my God, here she was, right on page thirty-nine, and there he was – Henry, her father – the two of them just variables plugged into an equation.

What had happened was this: she had failed – symbolically – to work through their mutual erotic attraction. Or they had. They had failed to acknowledge and renounce it. It was a kind of inter-ruptus, apparently, that had her going around trying to acknowl-edge and renounce it with other men. Only the other men weren't him, so it never worked. She was sure that, given time, she and Henry would've done it, the right thing; she pictured a primitive renunciation ceremony in which, through a gruelling rite of all-night dancing – writhing, hallucinatory, sweat-streaked – they exorcised their erotic attachment, emerging the following morn-ing from the ceremonial hut, irrevocably, psychically, sexually sev-ered. Into the Buick then, and he'd drive her – exhausted but actualized – to the gates of womanhood, where he'd drop her off with a mixture of swelling pride and empty-nested sadness, some-thing like the way he might have dropped her off at college had he been there to do it.

But that was the problem, he wasn't there. At crunch time, in the heat of the hunt, just as she was cresting adolescence, falling helplessly in love with him but not yet realizing it was all only a psycho-sexual construct that would eventually and inevitably end in her dumping him for a less incestuous love object, he disappeared.

Had she understood all that correctly?

She'd taken paper from the desk and with a blend of horror and excitement jotted it all down – finally! the law behind the seeming chaos of her life – but what was she supposed to do then? It wasn't like she could ask him to re-enact the drama. Anyway, how would they? There wasn't exactly a handbook on how, or there probably was, there was a handbook on everything, there was probably even a workbook you could buy, but that was ridiculous, and what if he was wet-brained? He certainly wouldn't be up for any hallucinatory all-night dancing, even figuratively speaking.

Her mind fills with unkind images. Whatever about unrenounced yearnings, she can still remember him – his flesh-and-blood, anything-but-symbolic presence – can still see him sitting at the kitchen table, late one typical night, his eyes lacking focus or even anything that looked vaguely like comprehension. His head swivelled slowly, a quarter-turn on his neck, as though he were a monstrous giant in the days of crude animation. He swiped a huge paw at thin air. His eyes swam and eventually rolled towards her and stuck there, like tiny silver balls in one of those hand-held games, rolling home to their little holes. She wasn't even sure he saw her, but she was sure he didn't recognize her. He didn't say anything, just stared dumbly at her until finally his head swung hugely back down again. That was around the time of the mailbox. When she'd stood at the kitchen window and watched him drive straight into it, not once, not twice, but three times. He kept backing up and ramming it again, like he was really trying to finish it off, but of course what he was he was trying to do was drive around it. It had hung there on its bent elbow for days, one of those pointers directing carnival-goers to the crazy house. He wasn't in any hurry to fix it, trying to pretend that it was something he'd had nothing to do with, thinking that if enough time passed they'd all forget and imagine it had been the result of a hit-and-run. In the meantime, the mailman had delivered their letters in a rather awkward crouch, and nobody'd said anything.

And then she grows kind. Because it wasn't all King Kong at the kitchen table or playing bumper cars with the mailbox. Sometimes he was more like Sammy, someone they should be nice to because he couldn't help how he was. Sammy was a slow boy they knew, the older brother of a girl she sometimes played with. Huge in his confusion, towering dumbly but insistently about the perimeter of their aimless games and gossip, which seemed lightning-quick when reflected in his sluggish, uncomprehending eyes. But then she'd feel bad, of course, thinking mean thoughts about Sammy, getting irritated with him. Because he couldn't help it, neither of them could. That boy's being slow was no more his fault than it was her father's fault that he was a drunk. He had a problem, right? He had a cross, a monkey, a demon, a weakness, a fondness, a propensity, a dependency. He was a dipsomaniac, for heaven's sake, a word she couldn't help but like. It sounded mythical and sinister. It was up there with consumption and the vapours, whatever they were. She thought 'dipsomania' and what came to mind was not shame or foul air or a dumb oaf at the dinner table, but people going round in hooded cloaks, priests swinging those thingeemajigs and little puffs of smoke darting out. It was a kind of possession, yes, and it was not his fault.

And even if he was possessed, sometimes he was wonderful. Like the day he drove her to Camp Hiawatha. Or almost did. She was ten. The big day, the big outing, her first real stint away from home. Oh, she had been putting on the brave face, acting like it was the only thing she'd ever wanted to do all her life, go to Camp Hiawatha like a big girl and hike and canoe, learn completely superfluous survival skills and have fumbling same-sex encounters with other ten-year-olds.

They made their way across Philly and north through Allentown, and everything was still OK, she liked having him all to herself in the car, he let her play her favourite Top 40 station on the radio and he didn't even care when she sloshed chocolate milkshake all over the upholstery.

But the Camp Hiawatha brochure kept flashing through her mind. Its upside-down horseshoe she'd have to pass through like a point of no return. Big horses that terrified her with their about-to-burst bellies, an indoor aerial shot of the mess tent – a hundred little heads bent over what looked like TV dinners – and the group photo of mannish-looking camp counsellors, a bad colour print that made them all look as though their faces hovered just a little to the left of their heads. By the time they got to a place called Weissport she was in tears and wailing *I don't wanna go, I don't wanna go to Camp Hiawatha.*

'You don't?'

'No.' She thought of the saddest thing she could think of, in order to call up more tears, which just then was being abandoned under that horseshoe in the care of those beefy women with ponytails and seeing her father speed away in a cloud of dust.

'Are you sure these aren't just wedding-day jitters?'

She was sure.

'You might love it.'

She was sure she would not.

He looked at her sideways and very thoughtfully, then put on his blinker and did an illegal U-turn in one of those spaces in the middle of the highway reserved especially for police.

'If you don't want to go,' he said, 'you don't want to go. And it looks to me like you don't want to go.'

She could hardly believe how great her life was! He didn't even try to talk her into it, he didn't make her feel like a baby either, in fact he made her feel very grown-up, the way he just let her decide like that, like she was old enough to know exactly what was best for her when she was not at all sure she knew, she was only sure she didn't want to go to Camp Hiawatha. She sat there in tense silence, afraid to say anything lest she say the wrong thing and cause him to come to his senses. She sniffled and pulled a strand of hair through her mouth, something she knew he found both revolting and irresistible. When he showed no signs of turning back and they were almost at Allentown again, she said, in the most pitiful voice she could muster and with an utterly false nobility, 'But you paid ...'

He just laughed. 'Don't you worry about that, chicken,' he said. 'There'll be enough chances to be miserable without having to pay for the privilege.'

Something's survived. So that his spirit quickens at the onset of spring.

He sees the external world aglow. Leaves a vibrant green, streams glistening, the sky a textured blue. He sees buds swelling on the still-bare branches and foetal shoots uncurling in the sun. He sees single blades of grass spiking through the churned stiff ground, with a resolve all out of proportion to their fragility. He sees seedlings quivering in the breeze, delicate and by a single frost dispensed with, and yet, like sacrificial antecedents – inch-high armies whose first advancing columns march dumbly into slaughter – continuing to come until finally some among them can survive, and do.

He watches as spring spreads itself, randomly and yet decisively, reclaiming its true territory or marking where home lies. He marvels at the inexorability of its advance, because for all its backsliding, its timidity even, there's a ruthlessness to it as it shrugs off its losses and offers ever more delightful reinforcements. And for everything he sees, Henry feels a sweeping and indiscriminate affection. Like being in love but with no one, and so without contingency, without the threat of loss.

He thinks of the seasons of his childhood, the years when he'd taken spring, unthinkingly, as his due. Happy, but never grateful, not yet knowing that the inevitable can also call for gratitude. And then he thinks of these past years, the springs that had hardly even happened. Devoid even of conventional charms (forgotten garden implements resurrected; children playing in the yard, reduced in the twilight to silhouettes), they'd passed practically unnoticed. He'd lived in his own microclimate, the autonomous inner weather of a cold sweat.

He can recall, though, a single instant (when was it? last spring, the one before?), the sun on his skin and some secondary lapse in his indifference, a nerve hit through a fug of anaesthesia. Though it wasn't pain he felt but something far more agreeable – light, heat, sensation – as shocking and as welcome as after the thousand rummaging unfelt fingers on some extremity presumed dead, the one arbitrary tap that registers. A tepid late-afternoon sun – warmth that wasn't there yesterday – glancing off him, beckoning, and he turning his face in answer. A deathbed dog pricking up its ears at the cue for an old and now impossible pleasure. Had he felt shame? Probably, but whether he did or didn't hardly mattered. What mattered was the feel of reciprocity, of something outside himself that bespoke light, and his own murky capacity to register the call.

It strikes him now as a tribute to stupidity. The fact he'd carried on at all. Strange, too, because his way of keeping going looked at times more like a death wish than an instinct for survival. It was a kind of power he was almost giddy with at times, a kind of high in itself – turning the sickness on its head and hounding it, seeing it through all the way to the bitter heroic end. (This, when he was just the right degree of drunk and life seemed a concatenation of elevating tragedies.) He imagined a death, suitably picturesque, his life unfurling like coloured streamers.

Now, he exists in the hyper-real afterglow of catastrophe averted, his most mundane perceptions resemble epiphanies, tripping over one another in their haste. Everything is rich and over-dazzling, as though he is under the influence of a hallucinogen which alters not the form or colour of things but only their intensity. (The tree line, the speared point of a fir, the gable end of the house, planes so sharp and angular they look capable of cracking off, fault lines he'd only have to tap to see the landscape cleave.) He is as though just let loose on earth – innumerable sights laying claim to his attention, all life at his fingertips and the world waiting to be named. His old, dim register with its limited repertoire of feeling (degrees of misery, variations of misgiving) rendered suddenly fertile, spawning a thousand runaway sensations. He sees and feels and thinks with an unfettered but arbitrary zeal, a kind of promiscuity of the senses that is not without its fear.

And yet he hasn't forgotten. Henry never forgets, even for an hour. In four months and twenty-seven days and through all this souped-up awe of his and whatever slippery way drink comes to mind and goes again, he has never forgotten. It is with him almost constantly, if only as a reference point, for his conceptual vernacular is still that of the monoglot: the drunk. It is the language in which he thinks and dreams and from which he must translate. It is the currency to which he stubbornly converts, weighing the cost of bread and milk and small extravagances against the cost of fifths and quarts and pints, clinging to the notion of it, that it might tell him the real value of things. It is the measure of each moment and everything he sees, the condition that makes a point of its opposite. As ill health does health, or winter spring, it is a life of incoherence that has enabled its antithesis to shine.

He feels the strange, and strangely comforting, sensation of having spent his life getting back here, to this precise state of mind. Of having gone from A to Z – this long journey of estrangement – only to arrive back where he began. He'd lived as though having been persuaded, in some timeless long ago, of this very moment. Right now somehow etched in him already, an impossibly prescient memory he could never quite dislodge.

This, then, is the afterlife, the afterlife he had ever imagined. Age-old now, he hovers as in wistful recollection of a long-abandoned earthliness. Excluded from any careless folly, incapable of true abandon, in possession of a wisdom he can't altogether welcome (more the incidental outcome of too much grief than the result of some concerted quest), he feels endowed with a weird near-angelic otherness that has nothing to do with proximity to perfection or a lack of sin, but rather with this bittersweet sensation of having been relegated to the periphery of human pleasure: he doesn't drink.

It's warm, even for the end of April. The steering wheel is slippery with sweat. She ticks the numbers off as they rise, odd on the left, even on the right, so his will be on the right. The streets are wide and empty, the houses large and solemn. Ancient-looking oaks appear at regular intervals in the green spaces between curb and sidewalk. A respectful, almost gloomy silence prevails. The sky is greyish-white and full-bellied. Nobody's out, and nothing moves.

She'd spent her last night (of freedom, it feels) in northern California, in a motel that looked like it was built from a kit, swimming slow lengths in the small outdoor pool. Around the pool's perimeter, chaise longues with pink plastic ribs and head-rests stained with sweat nestled side by side, slumber-party style. It was the kind of place crude tragedies might occur, senseless deaths. She imagined a nameless body going blue, a small huddle of dumbstruck strangers. In the distance she could see the neon of fast food, an Arby's or a Taco Bell. She played the surface of the water with her fingertips and it plinked like the high keys of an untuned piano. Somewhere near her, a generator rumbled to life, the sound of anonymity itself.

The rhythmic monotony of it calmed her a little, and the lap of water in the darkness. A sphere fastened to the pool's far wall sent white light, grainy and fan-shaped, through the murk. She thought of an underwater cinema, her own body projected, swimming in a mass of particles above a sea of heads. The light turned the water a deep blue, the blue of blown glass or curaçao. She swum blindly in the direction of it, felt the glare pressing on her closed eyes, spread her hands across its bellied warmth.

(The first time Jude looked back in a cinema and spied the beady eye of the projector – its lewd-seeming keyhole view, its cone of dusty nothingness beaming sneakily overhead – she'd felt swindled. Whether out of that particular illusion, or out of some more sweeping right to decide the where and when of reality's intrusions, she could not, at seven, have said. She was aware only of the fact of knowing more and feeling the lesser for it.)

She'd called him earlier today from a gas station on the outskirts of Salem.

'You should be here before dark,' he said.

From where she'd stood she could see in the distance a grey-yellow building decked with wire and surrounded by uncut fields. She was staring at it while she talked, shocked by his voice, which was so clear he seemed next to her; it wasn't until she hung up that she realized she was staring at a prison.

And it happens like that again now. Mesmerized by the climbing numbers that sit mostly to the right of their doors (their second digits slightly higher than their first, like notes in a music score, a homey sort of merriment), she does not immediately register the fact that she has seen him, seeing her.

On a porch, just up ahead and to her right, is a dark figure leaning forward over a railing, peering straight at her. It is so obviously him, she is filled with a sudden and unexpected sadness. For the offhandedness of it all. For the simple fact of his sitting there, of his having existed, somewhere, all this time. She feels herself beginning to sweat and it occurs to her to just keep going.

Instead, she slows and pulls up alongside a curb beyond his house and before she even has the engine off, he's standing there, outside the car door. She gets out and they embrace uncomfortably, their bodies at an awkward, deliberate distance, their arms crooked stiffly around each other. He stands back from her.

'Well,' he says. 'You made it.'

'I made it.'

'*Whew.*'

She has no idea what to say.

'I've been waiting' – he points to the porch – 'since this morning.'

She looks at the porch and back to him.

'You look, look at you. My ... God ... you look great,' he says.

'You too,' she says, though she is looking just over his shoulder.

'Well, I don't know about that,' he says. He peers into the back seat. 'Your things'll be OK here for now. C'mon, come up and sit down.'

She follows him to the porch and while he clears some newspapers from the table and fusses with the few bits of furniture, she glances around her.

'Here we go,' he says, turning, indicating two chairs he has placed at a companionable angle. But instead of sitting down, they stand for a moment, looking at each other before she looks away. He drops his hands into the pockets of his khakis, which hang loosely. 'I'm sorry,' he says, with a shyness that embarrasses her. 'I just can't get over it.'

He's smaller than she remembered, not shorter or even skin-nier exactly – he was skinny when he left – but there's a weird fragility to him, something vaguely elderly. His dark hair has hardly greyed, but it's thinned. Fine red lines, hardly thicker than strands of hair, flush his cheeks, though because he's olive-skinned the effect is less of dissolution than of weathering, like someone who's spent a lifetime among the elements. There's a certain vigour that hasn't totally departed, but it appears now to be skin-deep, for in another, immaterial, way he looks drained of something, some force or audacity. As though having suffered some monumental reproach, he wavers now in a timid uncer-tainty.

'What would you like,' he says. 'Coffee, tea, something cold, there's iced tea ...'

'Tea, I think.'

'Iced tea?'

'Sure,' she says.

'Coming up. Iced tea. Sit down,' he says. 'I won't be a minute.'

She sits in one of the chairs and feels a mild fear not unlike that which comes with sitting in the waiting room of a doctor's or a dentist's office. Of knowing pain awaits, or else the notifica-tion of future pain. She thinks of picking up one of the newspa-pers to distract her, but it strikes her as inappropriate.

He pushes his way through the screen door, the tray wedged against his flat belly. He bends at the knee and slides the tray onto the table and she takes one of the glasses of tea. When he lifts his own, she sees that he is trembling, and she's visited by an old trepidation. But his hands. She'd forgotten how she used to be in awe of them. The thick green veins tunnelling with a near-belligerence just below the skin, inappropriately visible and a lit-tle frightening, like tree roots erupting through the ground, his life support insufficiently concealed. She used to run her small finger up the length of them, pushing the veins this way and that over the raised ridges of bone.

'So,' he says, raising his glass quickly, not leaving it to linger in mid-air, 'cheers.'

'Cheers.'

He stares out past the porch railing, with a look that suggests he's never seen the view before. She diligently drinks her tea.

They have no idea how to do this. It feels to her like a cross between a job interview and a visit to an old folks' home, to someone prematurely incarcerated.

She nearly looks at her watch but stops herself in time. How long has she been here? Five minutes? Ten? She realizes that it had never occurred to her that there mightn't be enough to say. That such a long separation, instead of providing them with an infinite amount to tell each other (for how long would it take to explain twelve years by two?), has instead left a gap too big to fill. That maybe silence, if sufficiently prolonged, acquires rights of its own, and far from waiting eagerly or patiently to be broken actually refuses all incursions. That maybe there was such a thing in their case as a point of diminishing returns, some month or year when unbeknownst to them it had become too late, when absence had taken from them all the things they might have said to one another.

'How was the trip?' he asks. As though merely picking up a thread of conversation. 'Any problems?'

'No, no problems. It was fine. Long.'

'Well, I'm glad you're here,' he says. 'I'm really glad you're here.'

She sips her tea and, as though reminded, he sips his.

'And how are you?'

'Me?' she says. 'Oh I'm ... fine. Yeah,' she shrugs, 'Fine.'

'And Bill? How's Bill?'

'Bill? He's OK. He works in a real estate office.'

'He sells real estate?'

'Yeah. He makes good money, he lives alone, and he's, I don't know, nicer I guess than he used to be.'

'Are you close?'

She thinks. 'In a way.'

'Good,' he says. 'That's good. And your mother?'

'She's fine too. We're not so close.'

'Oh?'

'We don't fight. It's just, I think she thinks I'm not ... oh I don't know.'

He looks at her. 'I see. And how did she feel about your coming?'

'Here? Worried, I guess.'

'Worried. And were you worried?'

She is looking away from him. She swallows, but it's ridiculously difficult.

'Hey.'

'Hmm?'

'You shouldn't be worried. There's nothing for you to worry about while you're here.'

'Mm-hmm. Well, anyway, she's fine. She has a good job, she's an editor, of textbooks. She likes it.'

'Good,' he says. 'I'd like her to be happy.'

She says nothing.

'She deserves it,' he adds.

He reaches into the pocket of his sweatshirt and pulls out a pack of Camels. It's one of those zippered, hooded things like she used to wear in junior high school. When she'd looked up from the driver's seat and seen him in it, she'd felt a wave of disappointment.

'You don't smoke, do you?'

'No,' she lies.

He leans back in his chair, takes a deep drag and exhales, a long of stream of smoke shooting slowly through the air as he watches. She feels suddenly alone. There is too much to know, she thinks, and she's afraid of it all.

'Boy,' he says, turning towards her, 'I was so happy to get your letters. I didn't know if you'd even respond. I was afraid you might not respond at all. You know,' he says, 'sometimes I wondered if I'd ever see you again.'

'You did?' It had never occurred to her that she wouldn't see him again, even when she had nothing to go on, it had just seemed inevitable, unavoidable. And hearing him say that shocks her. That he'd considered it a possibility and gotten on with things anyway. She feels foolish and dispensable.

'Well,' he says, 'I wondered if you'd ever see me.'

'I never had the chance. I never knew where you were.'

'I'm sorry,' he says. 'I wasn't in any shape, I wasn't in any shape at all.'

She looks at her hands.

'I thought of you, though, all the time. Oh I know that sounds ... but it's true, Jude.'

She nearly flinches at the sound of her own name, almost as though he'd touched her. It's too much, his saying her name like that. She hasn't called him anything since she arrived. She did in her letters, of course – *Dear Dad* – but now that he's sitting beside her, it's too strange to say. She can hardly call him Henry, that'd be ridiculous, but to call him anything at all is a concession she can't seem to make.

'It's true,' he's saying. 'When I wondered was anything worth anything, did anything matter, I thought of you. Bill, too, of course. I feel terrible about Bill, but then I always did. Bill and I, even at the best of times, well, you remember.'

'Sort of,' she says, though she remembers better than he does.

He stubs out his cigarette and looks away from her. She is staring straight ahead, over the railing, the low gate, the sidewalk, to the house across the road which faces them with a spooky expressionless stare. Sometime, she didn't even notice when, it had begun to rain, gently, steadily, and now that she's aware of it she can't ignore the sound, it's like misery made audible and she wonders how he can live with all this rain. *Every day*, he'd written. Every day it rains. She thinks of him sitting here day after day, hour after hour, just like this, looking at the rain, probably not even seeing it, lost in his thoughts of God knows what. Her, he says.

'You know,' he says, 'I don't know if anything I can say will mean a thing to you. And I don't expect it all to be fine now, I don't expect that. But if you could just see, maybe, just wait and see and be here for a while ...'

They sit there, side by side, looking at the rain. The whole world, as far as they can see, dripping.

He takes another cigarette from the pack and lights it. He sets the pack on the table and she eyes it, then glances at him.

'You do smoke.'

'A little.'

'Oh dear.'

He takes one out and hands it to her, lighting it.

She smiles, barely, and lets her head fall back against the top of the chair, suddenly aware of how exhausted she is. She doesn't even want to speak, and in the sudden lull in her energy, in the brief rest from struggle, there is a moment in which it all seems suddenly arbitrary, how the way things are going is just one of many ways they could be going. A moment when she's outside of herself and sees, as though from a point high above where they're sitting, the two of them – woeful and confused and silent – and a small breach in the anger opens, a free space unburdened by any particular perspective. She feels a wave of pity for them both, sitting there, so small and far below her.

Just let it go, she thinks, let whatever's wrong go for now.

'This is a nice place,' she says, looking over her shoulder.

'It's very nice. I'm lucky. Believe me, I've been in some less nice places.' He sounds defensive. He doesn't want her to think he's been having a good time all these years.

'Yeah? Like where?'

'Like California. New Mexico. Texas. Nowhere's been very nice, really.'

'There must've been somewhere.'

'No,' he says, 'there wasn't.'

'Can I ask you something?'

'Of course,' he says, turning to her. 'Anything.'

'Were you scared?'

'When? At the end?'

'Ever.'

'All the time,' he says.

'Of what?

'Of everything.'

'Everything?'

'Banks, supermarkets, telephones, other people, being alone. Hallucinations. Scared of them coming, and then scared when they did come. And then nothing at all, just terrified of nothing at all. Just as if something terrible were about to happen at any moment, but only I knew it.'

'What did you think was going to happen?'

'Oh I don't know. Madness, I suppose.'

She looks at her lap.

'I'm sorry,' he says. 'Maybe you don't want to hear about it.'

'Maybe not. Not right now.'

'Sure,' he says. 'I understand.'

They sit there. The rain falling steadily, striking the ground in an incongruously cheerful patter. She hears him breathing, a sound she hasn't heard in years. A sound that, anyway, she never would have thought to listen for.

'I see something silver.'

'Silver,' Henry says. 'Silver? I don't see anything silver.'

'You haven't even looked.'

'Right. What about that porch swing over there?'

'Nope,' Jude says.

They're playing colours on the porch after dinner, the fourth evening of her stay.

'C'mon,' she'd said, 'I haven't played this in years.'

'I'm not sure I remember the rules.'

'Rules? I pick, you guess. Then you pick, and I guess. And nobody ever wins.'

'OK.'

'I'll go first.' She settled into the chair beside him, her knees tucked under her chin, her arms wrapped around her shins. 'I see something silver.'

It's a game he'd forgotten existed. They used to play when she was small, sitting outside after dinner, summer evenings. He'd drink beer and daydream and try not to guess the obvious. It was one of those conspicuously repetitive games that small children and adults can enjoy, but not really anybody in between. Now, it's just background noise to being with her.

Ever since this morning, he's been even more reluctant to let her out of his sight. He'd come home from the grocery store just before lunch. The kitchen bright with sunlight and sudden heat, the windowpanes still dappled with rain from the last passing shower. As he'd stood there unpacking things he'd bought for lunch, he'd grown gradually uneasy. There was an unnatural silence about the house. He stopped what he was doing and looked over his shoulder. The hallway dissolved in shadow. He walked slowly through the kitchen door and called her name, and almost at the same time was gripped by the awful certainty that he was the only thing moving in this house; she wasn't there.

He'd gone from room to room, first gingerly, afraid of the emptiness he'd find, but his search had quickly escalated to a frantic pitch until he was dashing up the stairs, calling her name. She was nowhere, though, and the silence that hung in her absence was so immense, so deep, he felt she'd taken more than just herself away, he felt she'd pulled the plug on everything, throwing his life and this house into sudden dark suspension. He'd stood at the top of the stairs, his insides, his thoughts, his feelings, all in that state of absolute arrest, the inner paralysis of grief.

He shuffled pitifully down the stairs. How could he have dreamed it would be otherwise? What perfect sense it made, what a fitting punishment she'd devised, lulling him into believing she'd come to be with him, only to sneak away when he'd grown sufficiently complacent, her sudden rude departure further shaming him for thinking she'd come all this way for any other purpose than to slap him in the face.

At the bottom of the stairs he stopped. What was he supposed to do now? Finish unpacking the groceries? Sit down and read the paper? Just what the hell did people do when there was nothing *to* do? Grief had its own kind of claustrophobia and if you didn't have a way out of, or around, or through it, it would swallow you up, you'd go out of your mind.

A tumbler full of iced gold alcohol drifted in from some recess of his mind and lingered on his mental screen, in dreamy levitation.

He went to the front door and opened it and stared down the street, in the direction she'd have gone. Even the street seemed robbed of something. Everything was paling, going dead before his eyes. Everything he'd felt the kindliness of – this house, this neighbourhood, the small porch on which he'd sat in every kind of weather, regaining himself – all of it barren now, and comfortless. Whatever he'd looked on these last months with affection or gratitude or wonder now desiccated because she no longer looked at it. It would've been better, he dared to think, if she hadn't come at all.

He rubbed his eyes and stared blankly up the street. He stared and stared until he realised that what he was staring at was her car, exactly where she'd left it yesterday.

For a moment he was confused. So certain was he of her having left, his first thought was to wonder how she'd gone without the car. And then relief moved through him. He saw her car there in all its mute indifference and knew, suddenly, how easily she could make a fool of him.

He closed the door and retraced his steps through the house. Upstairs, in her bedroom, he stepped over some clothes strewn about which, in his panic, he hadn't even noticed. He walked to the window overlooking the back yard and there she was, standing with her back to him, at the far edge of the lawn, where the forsythia was blooming. She was talking to Jean. Jean was running her fingers absently through the forsythia and with her other hand indicating, in a circular motion, the area around it. Jude nodded and gathered her hair and held it atop her head, her left hand resting on her hip.

Henry stared. Up to then he'd taken care to keep his awe in check, so as not to unsettle her, but now his eyes traced her shape with an almost greedy astonishment. His first untrammelled view of her. Grey-blues against the dark, damp mulch of the flowerbed, the thick brown hair falling loose from her hand, the slight list of her body. The grass glistened at her feet. Everything shone in the over-bright light after rain and an uneasy marvel stole over him.

She'd been eleven – or was it twelve? – the last time he saw her. The straight lines of her slightly gangly body, long arms and legs that seemed everywhere at once, draping in all directions when she sprawled in mock-exhaustion across the living room floor. Or the quick sprite darting out of nowhere into sunlight (for he associates her always with sudden light), or times he'd spy her in blank-eyed reverie, that strange child-stupor, as though in thrall to some fantastic inner vision. Days she still belonged to him, before she'd taken shape and deviated (less female then than an echo of himself); he hadn't been around to witness that, though he'd been long enough around to feel it looming. To see her body readying to gather itself, accrue flesh, tuck and swell, the convex-concave of her physical fruition. How would it have been watching his own flesh cleave from him like that, grow increasingly distinct and independent, that weird mitosis, the affront of adolescence. How would he have felt watching her grow necessarily secretive, even as her body acquired an over-whelming, even accusatory, aspect. For he imagined he'd have felt accused of something, adulthood maybe, or the desperate desire to keep it from her (this lost cause he'd have clung to), and he could imagine her rebuke, her brash physical refutation of his wishes as she grew inexorably into herself, and accordingly further from him. Saturated with hidden experience. In, eventually, on everything.

No, he preferred to remember her younger. A stick-girl on the beach, kneeling with a shovel in the sand, digging her way to the southern hemisphere while he read the morning paper. Summer days they snuck away early, just the two of them, alone then, in companionable silence (for despite her playfulness she could lapse into what looked like deep reflection – pouring handfuls of sand from one palm to the other or caressing a tiny patch of beach back and forth, planing it to a smooth windswept perfection), silence punctuated only by her random child-questions: why are there no waves in the morning? how come the water turns white when it curls? And then the sudden crook of her neck as she heard their names being called, her mother and brother trudging through the soft sand, the day having officially begun

She'd catch his eye then with a look of half-guilty disappointment, their mid-morning sanctuary violated. It was a disappointment she would forget within minutes, but what secret joy he took in it, in her brief, undisguised possessiveness. Her coveting him to the exclusion of the others, so that he felt he moved in a privileged hidden orbit around her.

He turned away from the window, awash in a mix of longing and relief. He saw her clothes, books, shoes, scattered about the room and felt the urge to touch things, her things. To lift her shirt from the chair back, her watch from the night table, to tenderly pair her shoes.

He shouldn't be in here, he knew, it was a mild invasion of her privacy. But he lingered anyway, allowing only his eyes to move over her belongings. There was a part of him that wished to keep her at a reverential distance – untouched, untouchable – as though if he did he could reconstruct for her some space, some undefiled past, before regret, before all this sadness took hold of her. Because it was like a weight she carried, an orientation rather than a mood. She moved in it, and he wanted somehow to disburden her, to stand far enough back from her that it had room to fall away, layer by layer, an original light let show, her self – the self he'd known – growing gradually discernible.

At the same time, he felt an equal desire to hold her, to touch her, to twine her hair in his hand. Not only to hold her, but to hold onto her. He hid his fascination, he averted his eyes. From the physical miracle of her being there, in front of him, beside him; he was agog, as though she were new-born or, more spectacularly, had risen from the dead. He saw her across the table and wanted to touch her, to verify her realness by feeling his hand meet the warmth of her own. But he didn't dare. So far, she'd kept an obvious (even exaggerated) distance from him. At night, she offered him a perfunctory kiss, but otherwise stepped delicately around him in what felt like carefully choreographed avoidance.

He'd looked around her room, with the odd feeling that he was mourning her.

'You know,' she's saying, 'I heard the strangest thing on the radio today.'

'Hunh?'

'I said I heard the strangest thing on the radio today.'

'Oh. What?'

'It was one of those phone-in radio shows and this guy says: I believe in the electric chair, my wife doesn't believe in the electric chair, but I do.'

'Mixed marriages,' Henry says, 'they never work.'

'No, no, no, you're missing the point. It was bizarre, like, do you believe in the electric chair? What is the electric chair, God?'

'In certain states.'

'Yeah.'

'Hey,' he says, 'I've got it. That bearded gnome down the street there. That silver garden gnome.'

'Garden gnome? No.'

'No?'

'Anyway, it was weird, and I thought is he just not using the right word or does the guy, deep down, really "believe in" the electric chair? Like the electric chair is sort of filling in now, for God, doing all the things God used to do.'

'What can God do that the electric chair can't do?'

'Exactly,' she says.

'Oh. Look. The lamp-post in front of that house.'

'That's not silver. That's grey.'

'Looks silver to me. I don't know, he probably believes in God already, I think I read a survey on that and most people who believe in the electric chair also believe in God. Hey, I know.'

'What?'

'The hood ornament on that red Chevy.'

'Aah. It's about time.'

'Now. I see something red.'

'The Chevy.'

'Of course not.'

'Do you remember,' she says, 'when I asked you how to believe in God?'

'How to believe in God? No,' he says. 'I'm afraid I don't.'

'You don't?'

'Um, no,' he says. 'I don't, actually.'

'Oh.'

'What did I say?'

'Well,' she says, looking away from him and down the street, 'you asked me if I wanted to and I said I did and you said that was half the battle.'

'I did? Gosh. And what do you think of that?'

She still won't look at him. 'I don't know,' she says. 'Kind of a cop-out maybe.'

'Oh, I'm not so sure,' he says, but he doesn't sound convincing. 'Because what's faith?'

'What's faith?'

'Mmm.'

'God only knows,' she says.

He smiles. 'Hey.'

'What?'

'You're not guessing.'

'Oh. Um, that red thing hanging over the railing there. What is it? A blanket?'

'Nope. Not it.'

'Hunh.' She shifts in her chair and says nothing for a while and he knows she isn't thinking about the game anymore. Finally, she says, 'What are you going to do?'

'When?'

'Whenever. Are you going to stay here?'

'I don't know,' he says, and says again: 'I don't know.'

It's getting darker, and harder to see. Henry feels a little cold. He thinks of her leaving, of how maybe she's been planning it ever since she got here, letting enough time pass so that her departure won't seem impolite. He shivers.

'Maybe we should we go inside,' he says.

'It's getting cold, isn't it?'

'It is.'

But she doesn't get up. Instead, she sits perfectly still beside him, gazing out over the street. He sees her hand on the armrest and wants to take it in his own. He wonders what she'd do. He wonders if there's such a thing as joy. Pure joy. A place he could lose this sadness, somewhere they both could. But maybe this is it, he thinks, right now. Joy, pure not because of everything it isn't, but because it's large enough to hold those things, to contain every one of its opposites. He thinks of how her hand would feel underneath his own – warm, solid, hers, enough. More than enough. In the gathering dark, he sees it clearly. What's left of his life ahead of him. The quick blue of falling dusk. Her hand.

Polygamy

He was flicking through a magazine in the staff room one coffee break when he saw it, in a small square at the bottom of the page, underneath an ad for anti-wrinkle cream.

He neatly creased the page and tore the little square from its corner. Folding it carefully, he placed it in the section of his wallet normally reserved for ATM 'advice slips', which, to his dismay, never contained any advice at all. He wished that just once the little banner would unfurl from the machine as from a mechanized fortune cookie, something homespun and true printed on it. *Buy a present for your mother*, it might say. Or maybe just: *Spend less*.

He thought that when he got home he would hang the little square of paper on the fridge, beside the postcard from Barcelona and the menu from the Balti take-away. He imagined he would chuckle at in a jaded, ironic way. Convert it to an amusing conundrum, a philosophical puzzle. He thought that when he composed his answer – which he fully intended to do – it might remind him of all he had to give the world, a little like a mother might.

But when he got home that evening, he saw it in a different light. It struck him as too challenging – too menacing, even – to be coming up against so often; it didn't seem motherly at all. He held it in the palm of his hand, wondering where to put it.

Imagine, it read, *that some future government has required all its citizens to provide written reasons why they should continue to exist, and send in your answer. (Replies limited to 500 words. Winners announced in February issue.)*

He shook his head. It was the kind of thing his ex-wife would have dreamed up to make him think about his life.

'You need to take stock, Jim,' she'd said. 'You really need to take stock.'

In the days that followed, Jim tried to catch himself in the act of being kind. He looked for opportunities to exercise his courtesy, his charity, his goodwill, to hand back change he'd mistakenly been given, to assist the elderly as they boarded the bus. But other than the proffered cups of the homeless, the addicted, the 'resident alien' (into which he made indiscriminate deposits), no opportunities arose; even the blind seemed terribly self-sufficient.

So he thought of arbitrary facts he'd stored, little nuggets of knowledge that might, when the future arrived, entitle him to existence. That Aristotle, due to a patriarchal blind spot, had failed to discover the queen bee. That there had once been a small shop on the corner run by a woman with only one hand. That his mother's maiden name was O'Donoghue. Or he recalled odd tasks he could perform, like peeling an apple in a single go. But by the time he went to write them down at night, they seemed trivial and embarrassing and he began to think of 'taking stock' as a cruel and unusual punishment.

Jim was a lecturer in psychology at a university in the city, a fact that seldom failed to elicit surprise. He appeared a little too guileless, too trusting, to have ended up trucking in the mind's deceptions, descanting on latent dream meaning and the pleasures of symbolic patricide. He looked more like a man you'd see mowing his lawn on a Saturday, a man you'd ask directions of, someone to whom you could entrust your dying wish, your unattended luggage, your daughter. He had a way of looking at people when they spoke, with a sort of childish bedazzlement, as though in thrall to their most ordinary utterances. He wasn't, of course; his mind being always and ever half-elsewhere, he had developed the compensatory expression of rapt attention. A dreamy lack of captivation masquerading as a captivating dreaminess. Women, once, had loved it.

Over time, though, they'd grown tired of it, and he had too. Where once he'd offered himself freely, he now required coaxing, needing always to be snake-charmed by his lovers. For how many times had he told the story of his life? And in how many ways? On how many occasions had he wished it were the final recitation? That the narrative stopped *here*, or rather that it become shared: a double helix rising through the air of his life, of their lives.

When he met Imelda, it did stop, or seemed to. Their embraces lingered in the air long after they had physically disengaged, so that the rooms of their home felt peopled with afterimages of themselves and he was always in the company of lovers.

She was a cognitive therapist. Later, he wondered if perhaps he shouldn't have fallen for someone simpler, a florist, maybe, or a nurse. When he was a boy, he'd pictured himself a doctor – a paediatrician (he'd never heard of neurosurgeons or oncologists) – coming home each evening with a boxy black bag full of coloured pills and magic potions and a stethoscope, to a woman waiting warmly to greet him. To a nurse, yes, nurturing and voluptuous in her all-white. (In his visions, she was always still in uniform, even while stirring something on the stove.) Very Freudian, of course. Unreconstructed too. But he was only a boy and anyway, the desire for unequivocal nurturing hadn't yet been deemed a gender crime.

When he met Imelda, there was no such thing as wondering about more suitable alternatives. He fell in love, and all arithmetic deserted him. He used to meet her in the hallways at college (she was a guest lecturer for one term) and he imagined the two of them as flowers blooming in a desert of explication. They would speak to one another in passing, as acquaintances on the street might – people who know only the most ordinary and innocent things about each other – and he would feel in these moments a gentle sort of anarchy unfolding. For hadn't the two of them discussed at length – in those more official, sanctioned hours in the cafeteria or the staff room – repression and projection and defence mechanisms. Infantile desire. Deciphering the psyche's codes, unmasking its tricks. And so clinically! As though such things had nothing to do with them, had no effect on their behaviour, on their fear of one another, on how close she could or couldn't come to him. As though they applied only to some other, earlier version of humanity, not yet wise to its own ways.

They were married in a registry office, to his mild disappointment.

'What about rites?' he said.

'Whose rights? Yours? Mine? The church's?'

'Not rights,' he said. '*Rites*. R-i-t-e-s.'

'Oh, rites. Rites are important,' she said. 'Absolutely. But we're living in a post-ritual world.'

'Not true,' he said. 'Everything we do is a ritual.'

'Everything? *Everything* we do is a ritual? Are you sure you're not thinking of a rut?'

'I know the difference between a ritual and rut.'

'Don't you ever notice', she said, 'that when people, people like us, engage in ritual, they always look a little ... sheepish?'

'Oh, I'm not so sure,' he said. 'Rites aren't only for the wronged, you know.'

She smiled. 'Perhaps they are,' she said. 'But it was a sweet thought.'

He smiled too. He didn't know if she meant getting married in a church or the joke he'd made.

He was sure they had been happy. Even now, he knew there'd been a time. It was a little like childhood, though, hard to believe it had ever been if you hadn't all those pictures to prove it. He suspected that when she spoke about their marriage now it was in self-deprecating terms, in terms of 'a mistake'. (The self-deprecation, of course, functioning as self-aggrandizement: how could she have been so foolish as to marry someone so much more foolish than she?) For he had disappointed her. He'd been a project that hadn't panned out. He got better and better and soon he was normal. But he never got better than that.

She accused him of bringing her down.

'You treat me like a drug,' she said.

'A *what*?'

'A mood elevator.'

He pictured himself climbing inside her, being whooshed through a dank shaft, careering through a psycho-vaginal darkness.

'Maybe I just know how to push your buttons,' he said lamely.

She had her back to him and was leaning over the sink, looking out onto their garden. Beyond her, at a point he knew but couldn't see, herbs perspired under glass in a warmth and imperceptiveness he envied.

'Jim,' she said, 'you're leaning on me. I can't take it.'

'I'll improve my posture.'

Why, why did he say such things? He knew she hated them, his little puns, his jokes. But he fell back on them because he was scared. In a childish effort to deflect the world that frightened him, he shut his eyes and stoppered his ears, thinking everything outside would go away then.

'Do you know what your problem is ...'

'What?'

'... your problem is that you want to be special, you want to be extraordinary and you're afraid you're not and so you've built this shrine to unhappiness and that, that is your speciality.'

He put his head in his hands. His elbows were on his knees. 'Are you having an affair?' he asked.

'Am I having a *what*, an *affair?*'

'Are you?'

'No.'

'No?'

'Believe it or not,' she said, 'I've arrived at this point of dissatisfaction all by myself.'

'I'd almost prefer you'd had help,' he said.

She stared at him. She didn't have to say it; she found him pitiful.

'It's not working, Jim. *We* are not working.'

He remembered that line for a long time, the one that made his marriage sound like a television set on the blink.

When she left him, he lapsed into solitude, and then into a torpor that would catch him unawares. He'd find himself standing in the middle of the kitchen, forgetting why he was there or what he'd been thinking or how long he'd been standing there. In an effort to avoid falling into such paralysis, he cleaned. The closets, the garage, the windows. He hoovered the blinds and the keyboard of his computer. He felt like a housewife from the '60s, or was it the '70s, fleeing discontent through a manic domesticity. He thought of valium and dexedrine and gin, he thought of symbolic castration. (Now *that* would be the very unsexing of me, he thought.) He watched every movie remotely watchable. Masturbation – which should have been a necessary evil summarily executed, on par with brushing his teeth – assumed an overly ritualized quality. He wanted away from himself, and yet recoiled from the scrutiny of human contact.

When people at work asked, he said he was fine, he was holding up grand, because any admission that he was otherwise would lead, he was sure, to he didn't know what. Men treated him with solicitude and tact. Women slipped him plates of lasagne or moussaka or spinach roulade covered in tinfoil, which he accepted with a certain wariness, as though they were tests of his sexual politics.

They sat themselves down beside him, looked at him soulfully and said:

'Jim how *are* you?

'Yes, how are you holding *up?*'

'Are you eating?'

'You really have to eat, you know.'

'You look like you're not eating, Jim.'

And he wanted to nestle his head into their soft laps and feel their fingers threading through his hair and, to the tune of some distinctly female music, weep.

At home in the evenings, he heated their plated dinners in the microwave and stood eating them alone, his hipbone against the counter, his eyes resting blankly on the floor or the far wall. Sometimes the sensation of it barely reached him, as though a kind of prophylactic sheathed his tastebuds. Other times something managed to slip through, a little zing of pleasure or recognition or surprise. He thought of the women who'd concocted these delicacies. Their respective predilections. Whether their offerings were traditional or adventurous. Whether what he ate reminded him of childhood or instead was laced with exotica from lands he'd never known or would know. He stood supping at their many tables, this nightly ritual the only form of intimacy he had, and it struck him as a kind of New Age polygamy. Virtual and primitive at the same time.

Lying in bed at night he listens to the shrieks of cats and the ripping caws of gulls. The cats mincing around the back garden, screeching with fear or desire or both, an animal urgency all the more urgent because penned within the city. He envies them their unashamed compulsion, their easily met needs.

He thinks of a note he'd once found taped to his door, a few summers ago when he and Imelda had sublet a cottage in the country and the cat that came with the place had run away.

Your cat is miowing in our garden, it read. But then whoever it was had crossed out 'miowing' and written 'miaowing'.

He'd smiled and saved it and when Imelda came upon it she found it as oddly endearing as he did and graced him with one of her rare beneficent gazes, half perplexed, half moved. Those looks that seemed to say: You are more than I give you credit for being.

One night, lying in his bed alone months after she'd gone, a cry he can't identify, repeated and repeated. He dresses, leaves the house and walks down the street and around the corner to investigate, imagining a dog or cat in agony, wondering if there is such a thing as A & E for the lesser species at this hour of the night. He is afraid to peer too closely into the darkened patches, afraid for the cry – which reverberates around him, everywhere and nowhere, like the ubiquitous alarms he's grown deaf to – to become localized. He stops a passer-by to inquire and his gaze is directed towards the corner of a rooftop where a single gull is perched, lost to its companions and weeping in a language all its own. The two men stand side by side in the darkness, their eyes on the small greyish shape calling disproportionate attention to itself, and a brief camaraderie passes between them, as though they are the lone witnesses to an unearthly visitation.

He can't sleep that night with the sound of gull. It's Friday and in a few hours, no doubt, he will be woken by singing, drunken medleys of easily remembered tunes, Frankie Valli or the Beatles. It seems sad to him, but then drunkenness does when it's not your own. Sometimes there are arguments too, men and women swiping senselessly at each other, and he feels like opening the window and calling to them: *Stop! You don't mean it.* Like the way he sometimes wants to scrape someone off the sidewalk and rebuild him from scratch. The way he wants to be somebody's miracle.

He listens to the rhythmic double cry of the bird and feels sorry for it for having such an unlovely call. He thinks of his mother, the way she'd kept a birdhouse out the back at their house near the seafront and tore the crusts of bread and threw them on the grass some mornings. Presiding over a small sea of pecking heads. He thinks of how it had unsettled and annoyed him as a boy – her nervy little friends descending, feeding in a panic before fleeing – and how now it is one of the things that makes him love her and feel sad for ever having loved her less.

He thinks of women and of how he thinks about them differently now. Of how what he misses is an intimacy as elusive as the climate of another season. The soft animal warmth of spring tentacling towards him through the deep freeze of winter – a desire that strikes him as rather disappointingly holistic – and he wonders has he lost the hang of something primal, that he can so seldom conjure up those old, crude scenarios.

Then he thinks of Imelda. The morning he'd lain with his back atop her chest, her legs folded around his own, the grim crackle of his cigarette in the grey air that looked more like dusk than dawn. Behind him, her invisible and trusted presence, guiding him blindfolded through the dark.

'Sweetheart,' she'd said, 'I want to sleep some more.'

He'd gone upstairs and made coffee and read a story about the circularity of time and felt all the while the fact of her beneath him. Breathing, sleeping, voyaging through dreamscapes while he moved freely and awake, as though entrusted with the monumental task of her safekeeping. Had his life ever seemed as whole as it seemed to him just then? Drifting through the rooms above her in a kind of exquisite peace, whatever was noblest and most gentle in him having risen to the quick. He set himself softly in the armchair and gazed out the window over the rooftops and the wires and the steel cranes in the distance. Imagining their whole house a ship, ferrying them to somewhere where everything was fine.

To say that he 'thought of' Imelda in the months after she left him would be inaccurate. It would imply that she gathered herself into discrete and recognizable bundles, images, words. That he could look into his mind like a microscope and find her there, visible and documentable; it would imply intermittent relief. Instead, she was as crushing and as formless as a heavy fog he moved through, stealing his horizons, his capacity for perspective, for taking the long view, inducing in him a claustrophobia that was all the worse for being without walls.

Other times he felt he was moving through his days, his routine, as through a strong wind. He attended his lectures and, on the advice of a friend, managed to perform by 'acting'. Acting as though he were a teacher. He could perform for an hour or two, but when his audience departed and he shuffled off stage again the fog rolled in or the wind kicked up and time stretched before him like a vast prairie to be crossed, with nothing at its other end but more time.

He attempted a cheap, comparative solace. Imagined himself cadaverous and big-eyed behind barbed wire and, steeling himself against his own minor darkness, said with shame: my grief is managable; my grief is First World grief.

Spring came. He walked the park, the squares of gardens, the Green. Sitting on a bench in the sun, he closed his eyes and attempted to align himself with all this sudden life. But when he opened them again what he saw was a world vividly green but sealed off to him, shrink-wrapped, like a ghastly display of supermarket vegetables.

There was a time – he could vaguely recall it – when the streets were seas of women and he used to feel he was presenting himself for consumption, when he'd imagined passing indiscriminately, anonymously, through the minds of women. He was amoebae, nutrients – an image gleaned, no doubt, from the Nature Channel – he was a million microscopic, deep-sea things moving through the filters of quavering, insensate creatures.

Similarly, he'd consumed. The entire litany of imagined pleasures compressed into the milliseconds granted passing strangers, so that he no longer had to think – and anyway, did not have time to 'think' – in order to live whole lives with women he'd never see again. Everything he was capable of imagining had shrunk into a single, habitual glance. Like learning to walk and then forgetting that one had ever learned, and just walking.

Now, they were part of the world cut off to him. Sometimes, he wandered to where they congregated and just loitered, lost, like a sad beast who'd got its mating dates all wrong. Found himself standing at the window of a hairdressers on Dame Street, watching them sipping coffee and flicking through magazines, hair rising in tiny helixes from their scalps, or folded into foil that cascaded in flaps down their heads like venetian blinds. Some he saw sitting under large domes that revolved in the manner of satellite dishes and made him think of alien impregnation. He thought that maybe in the future women would conceive like that, not with aliens, but with absent men. That they'd come to female-only enclaves and be ionized. Sex and procreation – at last – mutually exclusive acts. He wondered if one day people would just laser their way through life.

Walking away, thinking of laser beams and the future redundancy of touch, he feels tears pressing against the back walls of his eyes. He isn't a weeper – never has been – and is slightly caught out by his ignorance of its choreography. But as though guided by some innate grammar, he finds his hands rising to his face like comfort, like pressure on a suppurating wound, and when the flood subsides makes his way home through a stale underwater blear.

Once inside the house, he drifts between rooms, within an invisible but conspicuous occupancy, a vague presence that hangs in the air and is distinctly not his own. He feels a bustling, densely populated loneliness.

*

By the following week, he is no longer even wandering the streets, he is simply weeping. Waves of sadness move through him, so huge he can't believe he is the source of them. He feels the grief of ages, of whole peoples, of nations and disasters. He mourns a bygone version of himself, a self ignorant of the existence of such non-negotiable grief. He lies in bed, shivering, pleading with his unbelieved-in God, chanting mantras of naff self-help to keep his head from spinning right off its stem.

He gropes his way into the doctor's office, bent double at the waist as though suffering from appendicitis rather than misery, and is prescribed some rather sinister-sounding medication. When he is able, he buys a book and looks it up, along with all of its relations, each one an alphabet soup of x's and z's, all sounding to him like planets on *Star Trek*, or viral strains aliens would inject us with. Odd, he thinks. Odd that the little pills he pops to make him happier shouldn't instead be called something like *Summer's Day*, or *Your Very First Bike*.

He eats avocados and barley, takes B vitamins and folic acid. Takes himself, like a dog, for walks. He watches Laurel and Hardy. He forces himself to cook and to sleep and to use the telephone, as though enrolled in an introductory course on living. His dreams are vivid and disconnected and continual; their stories unnaturally short. Going to bed at night is like going to the movies but never getting past the trailers. Gone are the grand hysterics, the blotting-paper feel of him in which the sadness of centuries had crept through time to find him, in which perfect strangers had wordlessly declared to him their private griefs. The time in which he'd been as burdened as God.

With each visit to the doctor, he feels a little lighter, looser. He is capable of laughter and doesn't weep at all now (which, admittedly, after the excesses of the recent past, leaves him feeling oddly constipated). Over time, his laughter begins to mean itself again; each day a small skirmish that bit further inside the borders of normality. He presents himself at his doctor's office with a mild but growing pride, as though exhibiting an increasing range of movement in a once-shattered limb.

For a laugh one night, he'd done it. Dug the little piece of paper out from his desk drawer, assembled all the notes he'd tossed in beside it and smoothed a fresh sheet of paper before him. After several abandoned drafts and many intermittent lapses in his attention, he had written:

I do not know the rules of grammar, but I speak near-perfect English. This attests to my capacity for intuition. I oppose the death penalty and support the ISPCA. I am attentive in bed, or so I've been told, and I always phone afterwards, or used to. I am a man who believes in closure, in the mathematics of life [he thought such an attitude might be important to the future], *and I try to be kind where I can. I take public transport. I don't take plastic bags. I floss. I do sit-ups. I recycle and I Buy Irish. I have survived one divorce. I am able to surf the net and see through pretence and imagine ethics in a Godless universe. I am a morning person. I intend to quit smoking. Soon.*

He lit a cigarette and thought: I need to get out more.

The cranes were islands of merriment in the vast black sky; one a tableau of Santa driving reindeer, frozen on the verge of launching themselves straight into space. He walked beside her through the suddenly technicolour streets, talking about how the city felt like it was pretending to be someone else these days.

They were everywhere that winter, immigrants, refugees, strangers who might be either, or neither. As though the city were a dull rock that had been lifted to reveal a teeming underlife. Employees in the grocery stores spoke no English. The waiters were all sleek and Pacific Rim. Deep black men pushed prams alongside shockingly pale women. Gypsys (could he call them gypsys?) begging on the sidewalks, their babies in slings. Their vibrant layers of clothing rioting amidst the sombre winter light, the bleached skies, swimming against the current that washed over them: this monochrome population, cast abruptly into a grey, mean relief.

Everywhere, people looked taken aback, caught between wondering if they could rise to the occasion and wondering if they even wanted to. It felt surreal, and slightly off-kilter, like a black and white production that had been subject to the technology of colouration. They passed homeless people and addicts and drunks, who punctuated the streets like set pieces, Cassandras, allegorical in a way that both diminished and elevated them. They found a wine bar and ducked inside.

Her name was Nina and he'd met her at a Christmas party in a pub downtown, just an hour before. He'd been standing on his own drinking a beer and smoking a cigarette and wondering what he would do with his hands if he lived in a world without vices, wondering what parties would be like – would there be more touching, for instance? – when he became aware of someone shouting in his ear.

'Are you having fun?' she was shouting.

'What?' It was loud. It was always loud now. The world had become a loud place that he wanted to turn down. He was waiting for the definitive study on the rise in noise levels to be published. Something informative yet fun, deceptively amusing enough to domesticate the real horror of all this senseless racket. One of those books that turned big abstractions into small snacks.

'I said are you enjoying yourself,' she shouted.

'Not at all,' he said.

She raised her eyebrows.

He turned slightly and looked away, standing shoulder-to-shoulder with her then like they were watching a match. Every now and then one of them shouted a comment on the action. Until she looked at her watch and said, 'Do you want to go somewhere else?'

She slipped an olive between her lips – he imagined her teeth, her tongue, working the soft green flesh from its stone – and said, 'The gene pool ...'

'What?' He hadn't been listening. 'What about the gene pool?'

'... will we all just slowly get darker? Will there be such a thing as red hair a hundred years from now? Here, I mean.'

'I don't know,' he said. 'French people still look French.'

'True,' she said. 'True.'

He pictured the slow attrition of the local complexion, a planet full of grey-brown faces.

'You know,' she said, 'I read a funny thing recently. It said that the number of blondes in a given place rises in direct proportion to a rise in prosperity.'

(He thought of his vigil outside the hairdresser's and flushed.) 'Why?'

'Well, I assume it's because being a blonde is expensive, rather than because ... well, I don't know what else it would be the result of.'

(It seemed like another man's life.)

She must have misinterpretted his discomfort because she said, 'Don't misunderstand me. About the gene pool –'

(What had he been doing, really? Window shopping?)

'– what will be will be. It's just a curious thought, that's all.

The loss of certain ways of looking.'

'Like the loss of languages.' Rather proud of his analogy. 'What do you do?'

'Me?' she said. 'I'm an English teacher.'

'Really?' he laughed.

'Though when I was young I wanted to be a nurse.'

'*Really?*'

'Absolutely. Not just any nurse, though. I wanted to work on battlefields. I think I must've seen a photograph or a movie, I don't know, but for years I carried around this image of wading through bleeding broken bodies ...' – he raised his eyebrows – 'it sounds macabre, I know, but it wasn't. It was more about ... saving people. But without getting my hands dirty. I just sort of floated around making people better. It was all very vague really, it was a fantasy. Though I did get as far as looking up the Red Cross in the encyclopaedia.'

He pictured the two of them, him and her, in a parallel universe, healing people in a war-torn time. He didn't like writing bloodshed into his cosy childhood script, but for her sake he did it. (How odd other people's dreams were!) He looked at her: her black hair cut straight across her forehead and straight across the bottom just above her shoulders, so that he thought of a small box sprung open to reveal her face, smooth and neat and surprised.

'What?' she said. 'What are you thinking?'

'I'm thinking of you in a gene pool,' he said.

'Oh?' she smiled. 'How do I look?'

Not long after that, he showed it to her.

'Well?' he said.

'Well what?' They were sitting in his living room, drinking brandy, and she was looking at him strangely.

'Would you let me live?'

He was half-pretending it was all a joke, a little parlour game, though he wasn't sure she was taking it as one.

'You know,' she said, 'you didn't ask to be here.'

'True,' he said. 'But how long can I get by on that?'

She took up the piece of paper that contained his answer and studied it again. 'I don't know,' she said, 'I'm not sure you've put your best foot forward.'

'Oh? Did I forget something important?'

'Well,' she said, 'for instance. What about the stars? You know which constellations are which. And birds too, you can pick out birds. I can't. You identify things,' she said. 'You're a very good ... identifier.'

'Marvellous.'

'No, really,' she said. 'They're going to need that in the future. Because there's too much to know now. We're beginning to lose track.'

'So. I'll identify nuclear lesions and new strains of Ebola and forms of toxic gludge.'

'My,' she said, 'quite the little optimist, aren't we?'

He shrugged.

'What makes you so sure the future'll be hell?'

'I don't know,' he said. 'The present?'

'Thanks.'

'Oh I don't mean it,' he said quickly. And he didn't think he did anymore.

The dead of winter, and from his window he sees a single crane, stripped now of its lights. It hangs skeletal and ominous, like an out-of-season carnival ride. A night drill drones invisibly. Inside, he lies beside her, surprised, as always, by the weight of the human head.

His hipbone is a hard planed surface rising from the softer flesh around it. His haunches, when he rolls on either side, a diagram of man, muscle and tendon roped in red and blue ink. She kneels upright and pulls him to her and face to face on their kness they feel to him – or to her? it doesn't matter now – like two kids marvelling over a found treasure, a coloured shell or a bit of marbled agate. He unfolds her across the width of the bed. His hipbones knock against her own.

In the middle of the night he wakes and, walking to the kitchen for a drink of water, feels his body as though barnacled, with scents, residues, sensations still barely sounding in the quiet.

When morning comes, she's there, the suddenness of her an almost shocking confirmation of some dream-like, nocturnal visitation. She arches her back and then distends it, hooks her ankle round his own, pressing first one, then another, of the zones of her body against him. He bucks softly, sleepily, against her elongated form, and adheres to her with a semi-conscious certainty. Outside, in an early morning haze, against the grainy white noise of the city, a gull caws resolutely and is answered.

Snow

Every time Nathan comes home to Oregon, he is dogged by memories. Different ones each time. He never knows what they're going to be, but he has a theory about them. They're like dreams, he thinks, symbol-maps. Whatever fears he isn't dealing with, or decisions he isn't making, show up there, incognito. He likes symbols, the subtle relentlessness of them. He likes things that can never, really, be explained. He believes that when words fail people, it proves that every day, right under our noses, there are small mysteries being born. Things we have to take on faith.

This Christmas, it's ash. That week that Mount St. Helens blew and half the state was covered in a layer of light brown ash. It was the same week David LaMott died. Lost traction rounding a corner in the rain. His motorbike skittered out from under him and David skidded, on his side, down the street, as though sliding into home. Also the week Nathan lost his virginity. *God*, he thinks, marvelling at youthful resilience: *sex, death, an active volcano*. If even one of those things came into his life just now.

Maybe it's the snow that's reminded him. It hardly ever snows in Portland, but it's been falling since he arrived yesterday, the twenty-third. Like the ash, it has that same freak-of-nature feel about it, that exciting ominousness. Maybe it's death he needs to think about. Look at his father, the way his elbows and knees jut against the cloth of his shirt and pants, the old man in him straining to get out. And his mother. Years of breaking into exactly the same smile have worn lines into her face, around her mouth and eyes. When she is not smiling, her skin sags a bit, as though uninflated. He thinks of a lung, or the folds of a sail, waiting to be filled. Then there's this feeling around the house, as if an old aunt were expiring in the spare bedroom and any show of mirth, or health, would be considered unseemly. Bob and Louise – his older brother and younger sister – may or may not have noticed. Nathan doesn't ask.

*

It was Marie who decided they should do it, the night of David's funeral. They were downstairs in the rec room of her house, listening to albums, hardly even touching. Nathan wasn't thinking about sex, he was thinking about how the skin must have hung off David's face. *In a flap*, someone had said. But instead he kept picturing it intact, complete, lying on the ground a few feet from his body. Like when an android peels its whole fake face off and tosses it aside. Nathan's mind was that far away. So when Marie said, 'I want to feel close to you, Nate. I need to feel close to you. I think we should ... *do it* ... tonight,' the first thing he thought of was a suicide pact. Everybody was talking lately about those three teenagers in Indiana. Gunshot wounds to the head, their parents wanting to sue some heavy-metaller. In certain circles at school, Nathan knew, they were saying suicide was the only statement left to make. But he figured it was all talk.

'Do what?' he asked nervously.

She placed her hand over his groin. Her face was still puffy from crying. 'Have sex,' she whispered.

'Ooh,' he said. 'Oh-ho.'

He put his hand on top of hers and kneaded himself.

Years later, at the funeral of an old college professor, he had thought about that night. He thought Marie had intuited something primeval and he felt proud of them for having played their teenaged part in the great dance of dark and light. For having been eighteen and alive. He figured Marie needed to do something so irretrievable, so once-in-a-lifetime, that it would efface everything else that had just happened. That she could replace that pain with this one. Because there was pain when they did it. And blood and tears and disappointment. But at least this pain had a locus, and a limit.

Nathan hadn't known the boy well, not as well as Marie had. Nathan was a cross-country runner – a sort of poor man's jock – and Marie and David were heads. In the afternoons when school got out, the heads would get high at one another's shabby houses in Southeast, by black light, listening to Black Sabbath, Deep Purple, *Dark Side of the Moon*. Sometimes they ate hash brownies for lunch, right there in the cafeteria, under the principal's nose.

Nathan didn't like getting high. It made everything he took so seriously – himself, his family, his schoolwork, his future – seem ludicrous. Getting high made him feel as though he were being made light of, lampooned by life itself. Which of course depressed him. They could be out at Willamette Park, an indian summer day, sunlight bouncing off the river in a way that reminded him of a giant gold check mark – a big OK from God – and he'd just feel so incredibly blue inside. When he came across 'panic grass' in the dictionary one day, he though it the perfect name for marijuana. But he loved Marie. And there was something he liked about her friends. He can still see them huddled together at the funeral, crying on one another's shoulders, their blotchy wet cheeks pressed together. Not worried about the unattractiveness of their grief, the way kids in more select cliques would've been. They reminded him back then of photos he'd seen in *Life* magazine from the Summer of Love. Everybody half-stewed and draped over one another in semi-naked clumps, like forkfuls of fettucini.

Two years later, reading Chekhov in a coffee shop in the snowy east, he was reminded of them again, this time as though they were a pack of dull, uncomprehending peasants, railing stupidly against their collective fate. He felt guilty about the comparison. It wasn't even accurate. Because he thought that for all their lack of ambition, their glaze-eyed giggling, their stringiness, they were, in many ways, better than him. At least they knew who they were.

All that happened fourteen years ago, 1982, but it seems like lifetimes. This is a sensation Nathan's grown used to, without ever really understanding it. Almost as though he's been middle-aged all his life, as though he'd been born burdened. Nathan has never, if he were honest about it, felt young. He has never felt carefree, though he would be hard pressed to say what his cares were. He has had no great grief in his life, not one thing has ever reached into the core of him. He reads about floods, famines, street kids in Rio. He's got nothing like that to contend with. His life is Easy Street. He thinks he should join the Peace Corps, but only because he feels guilty. Only because he cares enough to worry that he might not care enough. Underneath it all, he feels like a fraud, and even that seems self-dramatizing.

Over the years, Nathan has been called: an old soul, a good

soul, a good soldier, a good egg, a good bloke (by a British exchange student), an island, an oak tree, a lonely planet. This separateness of his, this agonized solemnity, this inaction for God's sake, so often mistaken for depth. When what he wishes for is fire, outrage, a cruel streak even. He wonders if he has ever been truly disliked in his life. He thinks not, and he puts this down to a sorry lack of conviction on his part.

*

'I'm so proud of you,' his mother says to him, that night they are alone in the kitchen.

It's Christmas Eve. Through the window, he can see the snow still falling, the snowman the five of them built (with a forced spontaneity that made him cringe), buttery light coming from an adjacent window. He can smell cooked ham, cloves, the beer he's drinking. He feels nourished, and as warm inside as this room. Maybe he was mistaken earlier, he thinks. He could have been. Maybe there's nothing wrong. Who knows. Right now, he is sure of only one thing: this slow-motion, bursting-at-the-gills feeling which he has always chosen to call love.

She takes a sip of Burgundy, worries the hem of her sweater. It's chocolate brown, thick and nubby. The kitchen is oak; heavy saucepans hang from hooks above the stove. She has good taste, he thinks. She surrounds herself with rich, dense objects, though her preferences, her affections, seem to arise from a decisiveness that prefigures deliberation. It's not as though she has acquired discernment but as though she is these things.

'Why are you proud of me?' he says.

'Because you have the strength of your convictions.'

'You're always saying that. I don't even know what that means.

I don't even know if I have any convictions.'

'You're being too modest, Nate. I admire you,' she says, 'I do. Not everyone ...'

She flicks her hand in the air and trails off.

He realizes she is a little tipsy. She has assumed the quasi-philosophic bearing she so often does with drink, and she is pursing her lips in a way she only ever does with drink. A way that makes her look unbearably sad, when he is sure she means only to look pensive.

'It was the eighties, right,' she goes on. 'Everybody was greedy, going after the big bucks. But not you.'

'Maybe I'm too lazy to be greedy.'

'You,' she says, 'are not lazy.'

He tries to collude in her estimation of him. To believe that he knows what he is doing. That he prefers poor people to people with money. That he loves his life. That he is happy.

'What is happiness,' she's saying, flicking her hand in the air again. 'Doing what you were meant to do. And all the better if you're helping other people.'

Nathan cannot help rolling his eyes. 'I run a primary school,' he says. 'Not a leper colony.'

'You're making a difference, Nate. And it can't be easy, with those kids.'

'You're giving me too much credit.'

She shrugs. 'So let me. You don't give yourself enough.'

This is their secret: about love. It's not about more love. Or even a better quality of love. She could not choose, on a sinking ship, between the three of them, her children. This she makes clear. It's not exactly about shared sympathies either. In many ways, Nathan and his mother aren't all that similar. It's about blood, he thinks, and a person's soul. It's about being, somehow, both less lonely because she exists, and more. There is a strange rich sorrow that comes from witnessing her life. From knowing she is there, and beside him in the world.

'I used to love', he says, 'visiting you at the library.'

'The library! What made you think of that?'

'I don't know. Sometimes I miss it –'

'The library?'

'No-oh. The feeling. That feeling of, I don't know, not happiness exactly. I mean, don't get me wrong, I wasn't unhappy. It was more like, like a lack of sadness, maybe.'

'A lack of knowledge,' she says. She says this as though it were obvious.

'But about what, exactly?'

She looks at him, almost quizzically. 'About sadness, dear.'

'How circular,' he says drily.

'But it is circular,' she says, suddenly sure of herself. 'I can't define it, Nate. But I know what you're talking about. At least I think I do. And I also think it comes back to us.'

'You do, hunh?'

'Yes. I do.'

They can't define it. Faith, innocence, safety. None of these words would do. The memory of those days is irreducible. But also, nothing can be added to them. No discussion of their particulars could imbue them with greater meaning or resonance than they now have. Something existed – and was recognized – in its essence. A time. A place. A boy on the cusp of adulthood, beloved.

When they say goodnight, he presses her close, in a way he doesn't often do. (The feel of his mother's breasts against his chest is discomfiting, inappropriate; her smallness in his arms saddens him.) But he does so now, tonight. For her sake, or for his own.

'You're so good,' she says, over his inarticulate protest.

Unless he is mistaken, he hears her voice quaver. He doesn't let go, but squeezes his eyes shut tighter. There in the hallway, in the half-light, early Christmas morning, they stand embracing, swaying almost imperceptibly.

*

It was a branch of the county library his mother worked in three afternoons a week when Nathan was in high school. (His father was, and still is, an actuary.) It wasn't a particularly grand place – fibreboard carrels and countertops, white tiled floor, fluorescent ceiling lights. Nothing like the hushed oak rooms and desk lamps he found back east at college. But she was there. Standing warm and dry behind the check-out counter, her glasses on a thin chain around her neck, greeting him soundlessly with her small delighted wave. Her whole body like a hearth welcoming him home.

He had never, in his adolescence, gone to the extreme of disowning her, though he did, during the first shameful flushes of sexuality, turn increasingly inward and away from her. That he had to hide his new feelings from his mother made him angry with her. He felt her very existence a rebuke. As though it were somehow her fault, all this inconvenient and unquenchable desire. And her fault that it should cause him shame.

But he never lashed out at her; it was a quiet, downcast anger and it passed. There was nothing to apologize for, there were no real reparations to be made. And so at seventeen, he could seek her out and enjoy that rare blamelessness that her presence bestowed on him. She would motion to him, lead him to the stacks, to where she would have found just the thing on the Battle of Gettysburg, the Molly Maguires, Dred Scott. He would watch her fingernail trailing expertly across the rows of spines, scanning for the right call number. He liked her distance from him, her professionalism, the way they huddled under the hum of lights, whispering to one another about historical events, as though he were just another reader rather than her son.

After two hours of study, Nathan would change into his rainproof gear, throw his books in the back of her car, and run the six miles home. Out to the edge of the city, down along the river road and up into the west hills, through the paisleyed curl of the streets of his neighbourhood. Overhead, the trees dripped in the darkness and underfoot, the slick black pavement blurred past. He loved the rain washing over him, the knock and muscle of himself, the second skin of nylon on his thighs. He sang songs in his head or thought about girls or what he'd be some day. In his heart, he jumped from the pure joy of it. In the dark, in the rain, running, was as close as he ever came to forgetting himself, and so, to anything he might term happiness.

*

His brother Bob wakes him Christmas morning. He brings him coffee in bed. Asks him to deliver a speech on the State of the Nathan. This is an old joke, one Nathan has long since tired of. He wishes Bob could just say *How are you*, like any normal person. This way, though, Nathan's got to play along. Tell how he is, but only ironically, as though it were someone else he were talking about, someone who made Nathan laugh with all his shenanigans.

'Toss me those cigarettes, will you?'

'Tcth-tcth,' Bob says. 'Smoking in bed.'

'It's alright in the morning,' Nathan says, 'sober.'

He lets his head fall back on the pillow, and blows smoke

towards the ceiling. He hates himself for smoking. He vows to stop come January. He vows to want to stop.

'Well,' he says, 'as you know, I live in a log cabin. Purpose-built when the school was built. It's quaint, rustic, kinda romantic, but hard to live in and not think about Abraham Lincoln a little more often than you'd like.' He shrugs. 'Then again, maybe that's not a bad thing.'

'Might keep you honest,' Bob says.

'Just might. Um, let's see. I have no running water, it comes from a well. For heat I have a wood-burning stove. Sometimes I scorch my underwear when drying it.'

'Nice work if you can get it.'

'I like it,' Nathan says. 'For the most part. It's just, well you do sometimes feel like the world is passing you by.'

'That's because the world is passing you by.'

'Yeah. Maybe.'

They look around at the bare walls. When Nathan was in high school the walls were covered with posters of the Grateful Dead, Che Guevara, *Charlie's Angels*; a father wearing love beads walking with his son, below them in hippie script the words: *Take Time*. Nathan's own adolescence causes him to squirm inwardly. Its mix of slavish lust, armchair socialism and anxious sensitivity. He'd recognize himself anywhere.

'How's New York,' he asks.

'Full of money-grubbers and cokeheads and bitchy women. I love it.'

'You heart New York.'

'You better believe it.'

Nathan smiles, in spite of himself. On the good days, Bob is like a visiting spin doctor from a rival think-tank. A real shot in the arm. Everyone in Nathan's sheltered world is so earnest, so well-meaning, that he sometimes forgets people like Bob exist. There's a bond between them, but it's a once-off, dead-end kind of a bond. As though they'd been hostages together, or co-survivors of some gruesome air disaster.

*

They are outside, the three of them – Bob, Nathan and Louise – drinking mulled wine. It's late afternoon of Christmas day. They are exchanging theories as to what is wrong with their mother. Just a minute ago, they noticed her staring out the front window at them, ghostlike, then disappearing back into the house. These last couple of days, it's as though she's gone away somewhere, but left a part of herself behind, just enough for them to help themselves to.

Louise believes their mother is experiencing a kind of existential emptiness.

'She worked at that goddamn library all those years,' she says. 'Dad had a life. But she just had him.'

'And us,' Nathan says, 'don't forget us.'

'We were had,' Bob says, 'it's true.'

'Yeah, I know. But now we have lives. She has ... a house to clean. Wouldn't you be depressed if you were her?'

'That is so ... Betty Friedan.'

'Maybe,' Louise shrugs. 'But Betty Friedan had a point. In case you missed it.'

Louise is in her second year at the state university. She is studying environmental science. She wants to be an organic farmer, for a profit. Or else get a law degree, practise environmental law. Maybe both. She's like Nathan with a practical streak, or Bob with a social conscience. Sometimes Nathan feels like she is a part of him that got away. What he doesn't see is that Louise merely possesses a piece the other two of them lack, and lacks exactly what it is they each possess. It is as though, if each of them were to look at the other two, they would be staring at a blackly comic sight: the obvious but unattainable missing pieces of themselves.

Nathan is wondering about menopause. HRT. His mother's cervix and breasts. For some reason, he's convinced this is a female thing. His father has hardly crossed his mind, except to wonder is he aware of it, is he looking after her? When his father sits at his desk, calculating risks, lifespans, mitigating factors, does he ever think of hers?

'I wonder if she's sick,' Nathan says. 'I mean physically.'

The three of them look towards the house, as though it were the house they were speaking of. As though they were contemplating buying, selling, fumigating, or ridding it of radon.

'Well,' Bob says, 'if you think that's a possibility, then I think one of us should ask her. I'd like to know if there's something wrong with her. Physically.'

Their father comes out of the house. He's going to the store. For a second Nathan feels like they are in the waiting area of a hospital and his father has just come from his mother's sickbed. In fact, all three of them are looking at him, expectantly.

'Um, what?' he says. 'Do I look funny?'

He raises his arms and looks down at his body, in a kind of crucifixion pose. His three children look everywhere but at him.

'No funnier than usual,' Bob says.

'Thanks,' he says, and drops his arms. 'Anybody want anything?'

They shake their heads quickly and their father gets into the car.

'Don't you ever take a day off?' Nathan says, looking at Bob, sounding nastier than he'd meant to.

*

Nathan is elected. The three of them go inside and Bob and Louise disappear, as agreed. Nathan finds his mother in the kitchen. She's stirring soup with her back to him. There's a crossword puzzle lying on the table.

He puts an arm around her, loosely, buddy style, and asks if everything's OK. She turns in towards his chest and begins to cry. No, she must have been crying already. There is an established rhythm to her sobs. He's not prepared for this. He imagined double-speak, denial, a few feints, having to slowly draw her out. Instead, she is sobbing – freely and heavily – in his arms. As though she'd been just barely holding back, waiting until he arrived, until he made the appearance they'd agreed upon.

What comes to mind again is, for some reason, breast cancer. He imagines one breast, shorn from her body. Sun glancing off a long, thick blade. One fell swoop. He feels a tightening in his gut, a part of him that doesn't want to know. Because once he knows, he won't be able to un-know. Maybe he should tell her it can wait. Maybe –

'I guess you figured it out,' she says, pulling back from him, one hand covering her mouth. 'We've decided to go ahead and' – she motions with her hand as though she can't quite think of the word, it's obsolete, out of common usage, on the tip of her tongue – 'divorce.'

'Divorce?'

Immediately, he forgets her breast and remembers his father. He sees him cleaving from her. The image astonishes him. As though his mother were a self-contained entity and his father merely an addendum, tacked on in some forgotten era, for some now irrelevant reason. Strangely, now that Nathan knows what it is, he still thinks of it as something that is happening to her, and her alone.

'Oh I'm sorry,' he says. 'I'm so sorry.'

'I know we should've told you sooner,' she says. 'Oh God, you know, the whole' – there goes her hand again – 'acceptance thing. I guess we hadn't really accepted it ourselves.'

'I thought maybe you were sick,' he says softly. 'You're not sick?'

'No, I'm not sick.'

He hugs her. Her breasts against his chest. He minds, but he doesn't let go. He feels her heart beat, just.

'C'mon,' he says, rocking her. 'C'mon. Let's get out of here for a while.' He goes to the closet to get her coat and gloves. 'Let's go for a walk,' he says.

Outside, he links arms with her and looks at the sky. It's darker than it should be for this time of day. Snowflakes land on his lips, eyelids, the tip of his nose. Weightless, colourless, nonexistent upon contact with his skin; he wonders could it even classify as a sensation.

'Where is it all coming from,' his mother says, holding her palms flat up to the sky. 'It just keeps ... coming ... down.'

'Are you OK?' he asks.

'I'll be OK,' she says. And then quickly, as though she's reading from a script: 'I want you to know something. I want you to know that we haven't been staying together because of you. You all. We haven't been hating each other all these years. We don't even hate each other now. It's just ...'

He knows this is where he should shush her, tell her she doesn't have to explain, not now, not to him, he's not a child anymore. Yeah sure he wants to know. He wants to know were there others, was there cruelty, were there larger than usual lies? He wants to know was it ever really there between them – *it* – and if so, when did it die? And then of course: why? He would like to know how much pain, exactly, she is in.

But he says nothing. And he notices, despite all these unanswered questions, that an almost alarming clarity has taken possession of him. Maybe it's just pain, and the naming of a ghost. Maybe something else though, too. Not faltering. Being asked for something he didn't think he had, and yet finding it there, on his person. As though he'd been sitting there dumbly and along she'd come, tricking a coin from behind his ear.

She *had* been waiting for him. Maybe not at that moment, back there in the house, but this morning, and yesterday, since his plane touched down three days ago and for years before that. She has been waiting for him to recognize her. To come to her and really see her. And he has. If he can do nothing else, he knows, he can do this. Hold her on a snowy street in December, when her life has split apart. He can exist. He is alive, and beside her in the world.

Dust

It wasn't right, what happened. How they sat around the Christmas tree together and didn't tell them. How they swapped gifts and feigned surprise and couched sentiment in gentle sarcasm and never said. As though they could just skip that part without really affecting the plot.

The night before, they'd been to midnight mass – Helen, John, and their three grown children – attending in the spirit in which they might have attended a bake sale or church bazaar. With an indulgent, half-ironic wink, as though Catholicism were one more quaint suburban custom which, in their worldliness, they had outgrown. On the way home, the snow had fallen heavily, provoking in all of them a near-reverential silence that the service, with its jostling and acrid smell of drink, had not. As the car moved smoothly through the white streets, Helen saw split-rails, lamp-posts and bike racks, their sharp points rendered soft, and felt an air of mutability attaching to the truth.

Bob suggested building a snowman and his father floodlit the yard, so that it shone a sunny yellow. Bob and Nathan and Louise started rolling balls of snow, their suddenly purposeful activity like that of people mobilized in a crisis. The glowing tips of cigarettes waved about by their gloved, gesticulating hands made their mother think of lightning bugs. Some miraculous mid-winter visitation.

Helen felt herself an almost objective witness to the proceedings, as though the project were less an off-the-cuff response to snowfall than a sort of Rorschach test. And she waited, curious, to see would what shape the snow would assume.

'I motion,' Nathan said, 'we call him Frosty.'

'Frosty?' Louise said. 'Kind of corny.'

'Exactly. *Not*.'

'Ooh,' Bob said, 'I get it. Like we're ... beyond corny. We're post-corny.'

'Post-that, even,' Nathan said. 'Which is why we can call him Frosty without succumbing to either dopey naïveté or bitter irony.'

'Hear, hear.'

'Is it possible', Louise said, 'to be post-ironic?'

'It is,' Bob said, 'but ...'

'Here we go ...'

'... then you'd be a mailman in Athens.'

'Brrrrbb-Tchuu!' Nathan struck an imaginary cymbal.

Helen wished her children wouldn't talk like this. She felt strangely undermined by their irreverence; she took it personally. She knew that when they talked about dopey naïveté, they were referring to that era in which she would have been just about the age Louise was now. When they would have named a snowman Frosty without having to deconstruct the impulse. But everything with them was doublespeak, at least.

'I motion,' she said cheerily, 'that we go inside.'

'Good idea,' John said. John. She'd forgotten he was there.

Inside they compared airline food, and Nathan described, with disproportionate passion, something new he'd discovered you could do with sage. Then a discussion she couldn't follow about red meat and acids and arthritis. Nathan had recently become a vegetarian.

'I don't know what you're worried about red meat for when you're smoking those,' John said, pointing to the butts in the ashtray.

'I know, I know. But that's not the only reason, my health, it's you know, immoral. Killing animals.'

'You a Buddhist?' Bob asked.

'*Are* you a Buddhist?' Louise said.

Nathan squirmed visibly. 'Well,' he said, 'I've been doing a bit of, a bit of Buddhism alright, yeah.'

'A ... bit ... of ... Buddhism,' Bob said. 'Hunh. I've heard of à la carte Catholicism.'

Nathan noticed his father eyeing him suspiciously, as though waiting on the admission of some further perversion. Homosexuality, perhaps, or nipple-piercing. It was strange, when Nathan was alone or with friends or even with a woman, he felt fine: physical, substantial, masculine enough. He was strong, after all, and tall, his musculature pulled taut over the rack of his frame. But in the presence of his father, he felt lacking in density. Wispy, inconsequential. As though he were somehow letting down the side.

'So what do you do,' his father said. 'Do you ... meditate ... or what? What does a Buddhist do?'

'I'm not a Buddhist,' Nathan sighed. 'I'm just investigating.'

'But I'm asking. Like, what makes someone a Buddhist? As opposed to –'

'As opposed to, say, a travelling salesman,' Bob said.

'The practice of Buddhism,' Nathan said, ignoring his brother. 'Obviously.'

'Oh boy.' His father clapped his palms to his thighs. 'We're getting nowhere. Why so defensive, Nate?'

'John.'

'What, I'm only asking.'

'Drop it,' Helen said. 'It's his business.'

'Funny timing, that's all,' he went on. 'He picks Christmas Eve to tell us he's not a Christian anymore. Not that I mind. It's his life.'

'I agree with you there,' Louise said. 'Religion's really personal. It's like being gay or something. Nobody else's business.'

John looked at Louise. Nathan smiled. Now his father thought Louise might be that way too. Even Bob was silent.

'Oh God,' Louise said, rolling her eyes. 'I was just making a point. Lighten up, Dad. You too, Neanderthal.'

'Like you said, it's nobody's business. I'm just marvelling', Bob said, 'at the profundity of your observations. Religion is like being gay. In terms of promiscuity, I assume you mean.'

'You know what I mean,' Louise said. 'It's personal. Only you can choose your religion.'

'I beg to differ with you. If there're two things in this world that are not personal, they are religion and sex.'

'Well, they should be.'

'Ah, that's different.'

'I think,' Helen said, 'it's that time.'

'Yeah,' John said, though he hadn't taken his eyes off his daughter.

*

While John and Louise and Bob headed for bed, Nathan helped his mother carry beer bottles, wine glasses, ashtrays into the kitchen. She could've told him then. There had never been any small talk between the two of them, nothing she'd had to get beyond, or beneath, to reach him. But she didn't. Instead, they talked of the past. Nathan seemed keen to reminisce and almost puzzled by the fact. Sitting in the kitchen with her son, Helen had the odd – though not completely alien – sensation that it was he she was married to. That the two of them might easily be sitting around after a party, husband and wife, performing a postmortem on the evening, or on their own lives. But when they said goodnight and she embraced him, he felt – despite his size – so young to her.

John didn't stir when she climbed into bed, but she knew he was awake. 'It's Christmas,' she said into the darkness.

'Mmm.'

'Christmas.'

'Go to sleep, Helen.'

She found that lately, what she'd acquired in place of the pain was a certain philosophical remove. As though this marriage had been a bold new experiment in living, and this not so much its tragic end as the point at which they sat back and analyzed the data. What was its natural lifespan? By what conceivable means might that be extended? The appearance of children, perhaps, or their reappearance at seasons of peak sensitivity. We are cosmonauts, she thought, stepping bulkily out the hatch of our spacecraft, filled with yarns from the beyond. Well. You get through it how you can.

What John would say is this: What I don't get, he'd say, is why love dies.

While what baffled her was not that it died, but how quickly and with what apparent ease. True, they'd been together for more years than most, but she could count on her fingers those first pristine days. When they'd known just enough about each other to insist on knowing more. Why?

Why that dumb, blind insistence on knowledge, that belief that it'd be good for you? And then, of course, there was another question. What did you do with what you knew? That's what makes or breaks you, Helen thought. Because it seemed to her that this was not stupid – this insistence on participation in a life that was bound to disappoint you – but indomitable. What was stupid was avoiding knowledge, or pretending not to have it. Imagining you could strip away the dross and get at that shining thing you once were.

You needed, she knew, those first days, in order to come as far as you have. But you shouldn't need them back.

*

'But where does it come from?' John was saying. 'I mean, what makes dust?'

That day, so soon into their marriage, when she'd asked him for help around the house. He'd gone over the room, running his index finger along flat surfaces, pressing and rolling the dust between his thumb and first finger, apparently aghast.

'Hunh,' he'd said. 'Hunh.'

'Give me the rag,' she'd said finally. Exasperated, but not exactly nasty.

'No, I just –'

'I'll do it,' she'd said.

She felt sent-up, patronized. But is it possible she mistook his tone? What if, instead, she'd indulged him, gone along with his half-real, half-put-on amazement. Called his bluff, as it were. She might have written his name with her finger on the dusty mantel and then slowly, teasingly, pushed the rag across it. As though, just like that, she could forget his name. She might have talked of earth, or death. Sunbeams. Snow on the shoulders of his over-coat. The word *motes*. She wouldn't, in the end, have been able to answer his question, but this he would not have noticed. Because an answer wasn't exactly what he was looking for. Because John, at that time, was still capable of a wide-eyed curiosity, and all he really wanted just then was a little company in his wonder.

But let's not blame Helen. What did she need? She might have needed to know that these flights of fancy didn't mean he wasn't rooted there, with her. That they could even include her. In order to stop pulling him back, she needed to know he wasn't going anywhere. And it wouldn't have cost him much, really, just to say to her: I'm here.

*

There is not much time left in this marriage. Two weeks, maybe three. A month if they soften. They'll survive the New Year, with all its mandatory melodrama. They will get saddeningly, neces-sarily drunk. At a party, they will somehow summon up the energy to engage in the usual round of tired flirtations. It's possi-ble there will be one or two old lovers there, on his side or on hers. These people will appear to them as old photographs of themselves sometimes do. At midnight, John and Helen will embrace and one of them – it's hard to say which – will say *I'm sorry*, just as the other one is saying *Happy New Year*. In the midst of this embrace, they will feel they are holding tight to their secret and for this reason they will find it hard to let go. It is, they'll know, the last secret they are ever likely to share.

They won't fight. They are beyond fighting. But in the taxi on the way home they will slip into a morose silence, and an image will present itself to Helen. It is of January, people going their separate ways. Like the cast of a play after an unusually long and surprisingly successful run. Already there's that sense of depletion, extrication. Of being not in the moment, but a step ahead of it.

But that's a few days down the road. Right now, it's Christmas, and waking up this morning Helen and John realize what a disastrous idea this was, this gathering of their clan, how finely they've tuned their masochism.

There is a knock on the bedroom door, a complicated one. It's a Christmas carol, but unrecognizable. Rhythm was never in the genes.

'Are you decent?' Bob asks. 'Can we come in?'

'We're decent,' John says.

Louise is carrying a tray, with toast and coffee and freshly squeezed juice. Bob has taken two balls from the tree and hooked them on his ears.

Helen rolls her eyes at him and smiles. 'Where did we get them,' she says to John.

'Don't worry,' Bob says, 'we're only the warm-up act. There are tassel-breasted women waiting in the yard.'

'Not again,' John says.

'I'm afraid so.'

Louise and Nathan stand waiting.

'This is so ... sweet,' Helen says. 'This is so sweet of you.'

'It was my idea,' Louise says.

'Was not.'

'Was too.'

'The breakfast,' Nathan says with undue solemnity, 'was Louise's idea.'

'Thank you, dear,' his sister says.

Helen looks at Nathan, her middle child. This odd sense of responsibility he bears, even in the midst of jesting. She lets wash over her a truth which normally she keeps at bay. That she loves him more than the other two. Or at least more instinctively. His depths, his way of looking at her, as though for answers. His heaviness of heart, which she's never understood the source of, but which she feels like a weight on her own shoulders.

'I think I'm going to cry,' she says blankly.

'Oh dear,' John says.

'Mom ...'

'I hate to see a woman cry,' Bob says.

'Come on,' Nathan nods towards the door. 'Come out whenever you're ready.'

They file out, closing the door behind them and she does cry. But only briefly. Very quickly, she is empty, and her sobbing feels almost staged. As though she has cried on cue and can stop now. John lifts the tray and clears a space for it on the nightstand. He rocks her briefly and, when her tears cease, withdraws.

'I never thought it would be like this,' he says.

Oh God, she thinks bitterly. She hates it when people say that. What's *it*, anyway? Their lives? Their marriage? Getting old? This morning? Grow up, she feels like saying. Wake ... the ... fuck ... up.

'You never thought *what* would be like *what*?' she says.

'I never thought I'd feel so ...'

'So what? Ashamed?'

'Can I speak? Please.'

'Speak,' she says, 'speak. By all means, speak.'

'This wasn't my idea, if you recall.'

'My apologies,' she says slowly, 'for having had an idea.'

'Oh don't give me that.'

She flounces – that's the only word for what she does – she flounces about the bed. It's the only movement that comes close to expressing her exasperation with him. With his need to assign blame. With his sudden passivity when things go wrong.

'If it was my idea,' she says, 'it was because I thought it might ... oh ...'

'Work?'

'Help.'

'Did you?'

'Did *you*?'

Go on, she thinks, say it: *I asked you first*.

Instead, he softens. Seems to crumple almost, there in the bed beside her. But not in the usual way, the way that begs her sympathy, makes her feel a hammer to his anvil. He sags perceptibly.

She wants him to say it's over. Or a part of her does. To bump them free of this groove they're in. To say it doesn't matter whose idea it was – this Christmas, this life, this whatever it is they're trying that so obviously is failing. She would like him to admit that this plan has grown heads, and that what he wants more than anything right now is just to give up.

But he won't say it. She knows that.

'I don't know what I thought,' he says finally. 'I honestly don't know.'

In the old days, she knows, you held back because you cared. And in the even older days you didn't have to hold back, because the stuff just wasn't there, there was no scorecard yet. You made untold allowances for each other's feelings. You hardly even knew you did it and you certainly never mentioned it. But pretty soon you wanted credit for all those allowances you'd made and from there it was only one step to the place where you just didn't make them anymore.

He is sparing their feelings, even at this late stage. They might be beyond crying, but they are also beyond cruelty. What the kids might call *post-caring*. Where it doesn't matter that it doesn't matter anymore.

She rises from the bed and looks down at him. Something passes between them, something centuries old and not altogether bad: honour in the admission of defeat. They feel unconscionably heroic and, strangely, free.

She takes her robe from its hook and shuts the bathroom door behind her. On the nightstand the coffee's gone cold. John looks at it wistfully, and not without guilt. As though it were someone's school project he'd let fall behind the fridge, and then forgotten.

*

Their gifts to one another this year are, as if by prior arrangement, empty of any suggestion of the future. Of anything they might share in or admire on one another or build upon together. Gone are the silk scarves of other years, anything in that colour she so loves on him, a vase to hold the flowers he is prone to buying each January, to embolden the grey days ahead.

They exchange instead the obligatory, generic gifts of near-strangers. Best-sellers rather than the leather-bound volume she'd coveted from the old book stall. A new grip for his racquet rather than his favourite hand towels, which would one day smell of him. Nothing that might reveal what they know of one another's more intimate but less pressing needs. The kids don't notice. But that's the nature of intimacy. That it has its own symbols, which other people can neither read nor read the absence of.

*

Late that afternoon, Helen sits at the window, watching. The air is dark blue, the forecast for more snow. Bob and Nathan and Louise are standing outside, drinking hot spiced wine. Written on their faces is ease. Now and then, one of them will form a snowball and heave it in someone else's direction. Half-heartedly and with no malice. Bob and Nathan smoke. Louise, no. Not yet, anyway. In the end, Helen thinks, there's very little we can protect them from.

Bob is waving one arm, then pointing skyward. He's telling a story. About what, Helen cannot imagine. But it's making Louise laugh and Nathan shake his head and smile. They seem to Helen so worldly and at home in themselves. She was never like that. Nor, she thinks, was John. Her kids will make mistakes, she knows, perhaps big ones, but the difference is, they will expect to make them. They know too much. About economic miracles, the reinvention of individuals and societies; what, out there, is worth saving, and what we only cling to out of fear. Very little will strike these three as cataclysmic and that seems to Helen both a blessing and a deprivation. The moon to them is just a place you go if you're very smart and very fit and certifiably sane.

She attaches colours to each one of them. Louise is all earth tones, that's easy. Olive green or rich browns. Nathan is sea-blue, but not Caribbean. More dense and still and deep; a latent sort of power. And Bob is like the fierce non-colour of a star. Constant, and though first, the furthest from her. He buys and sells money for a living. What does that even mean? She has heard him speak of people losing millions, but only on paper. Helen doesn't understand, nor does she want to. She can't help thinking it a gross inversion of the natural order, when you're not even buying products anymore, but money with your money. And yet he is still Bob, her son. Capable of gruff but genuine affection, and a sense of loyalty that precludes analysis. Certain things just are with Bob. He will never understand her, and he knows that, but he will come to her if she needs him.

Nathan teaches poor kids. Underprivileged, she means. She keeps picturing him on a reservation, though she knows he lives in a small log cabin in the Appalachians, happy it seems. This is his choice, though it could change tomorrow. Change to them is a byword, and no cause for alarm. He, above them all, seems in search of something. Louise, less so, but then she's young, only twenty. Lately, she's been talking all the time about Gaia. She tells Helen about the earth and the trees and the flowers and how they all have souls and that only when we accept this can we move beyond this ethos of destruction. She can say this only because she is aware of large-scale destruction, a fact that fills Helen with both envy and regret. This is not her final form, of course. Louise will live through many incarnations. But it's an indication of where, already, her sensibilities lie.

Louise is seated on the hood of the car now, and Bob and Nathan on the low brick wall that contains the flower-beds. She's explaining something and they are listening, intently. That's another thing. That Louise is not shy of them. She apologizes, apparently, for nothing. Not her youth or her sex or whatever statistical information or hard data she may lack. She believes conviction will carry her. And Helen knows these things are so because of Bob. He set a tone, one lacking in apology or fear, which his sister has adopted and refined. Aside from that, Bob loves Louise. More, Helen knows, than he loves Nathan. And, likely, more than Louise realizes at her age. Helen knows she owes Bob a debt of gratitude, but still there's this discomfiting sense of distance between them. As though he were a man she knew only in passing, who has delivered her children home safely from summer camp, having taught them the rudiments of survival.

Something fine is taking shape before her. In spite of her, in spite of John. And what the two of them have tried to do is milk that – extract from it some faith or future – and how shameful and transparent their efforts feel. Out there lies proof of certain things. That they lived and loved each other and procreated. That there were other, better times, the fruits of which are out of reach now, as lost to them as the times themselves. Helen and John move about on the perimeter of all this in an almost funereal fog, as though they have swum, spawned, and are dying.

She knew today what John wanted. To turn back time, and then stop it. If there was to be an apotheosis, it would have come this morning. In bed or opening presents, with their children at their feet. As though they might wake Christmas morning to find themselves feeling, for the first time in so long, included in their own lives.

But what has instead come clear to them is exactly the opposite of what they'd sought. The separateness from them of their children is so starkly obvious. She and John are at the centre of nothing; they've been left behind. They're in the queer position of people who, knowing they're dying, have thrown a farewell party for their friends. But not wanting to spoil anything – wanting their loved ones unburdened and spontaneous around them – they have kept their secret, and thus sidelined themselves from any joy. They can count on these people neither to revive them, nor, for any length of time, to mourn their passing. They can't even count on shock. It may not come.

Here, Now

Out here, where home is – 12 miles from town, 132 from the capital, latitude 54 degrees 20 minutes, longitude 8 degrees 40 – we're at the centre of our universe. Our peninsula: tiny feline tongue-flick into the endless liquid of the Atlantic. *Cape Neurotic, breakaway republic, bandit country* – all pet names, only the first of which I've ever understood. Much further north and you're AWOL, into the too-high wilds of Donegal. But here, despite the silence, we seem not too far from anywhere. Silence that sometimes – like a climber's nightmare, a hidden cleft – feels like the firm earth having suddenly given way beneath us, dropping us irretrievably into dark and hollow. Only an illusion; we're on solid ground here. Nestled between mountain and shoreline, or rise and fall, able anytime to look left, or right, and be shown what it is we're relative to.

From where we are (as from a lot of places now), the new highways radiate like spokes from the hub we imagine *here* is, drilling past the now redundant, serpentine old laneways (recall: the shock of rod and spiral, side-by-side on the small slide, your very first turn at the microscope). Suggestion of stark choice, between what demands but rewards, and the line of least resistance. Roads hastening us in three directions, towards Galway, Dublin, Donegal. Roads referred to not by name but by order of appearance: Old and New. As though there would only ever be two versions of a thing, or ever one definitive account.

SUMMER

Reneged-on promise, spring's failure to deliver, *coitus interruptus* of a season. Worse somehow than winter, which, at the very least, arrives. I haven't learned it, the fine art of pessimism. How to stop expecting. *Teach me*, she wrote, before departing, *what I have to have to live in this country*.

THE NEW ROAD

Which you and I didn't live to see. Lying in your upstairs bedroom all that dank summer of its construction, its tripartite beat tripping off our tongues. Eight-point-eight kilometres of sudden superhighway and right outside your door. The changes it would bring! As though it were the coming of the motor-car itself. Here to there in no time flat; what we couldn't do with a proper passing lane. How what for eons had been villages would overnight begin to feel like 'suburbs'. We hadn't much else to talk about, which doesn't mean they weren't good nights.

Autumn, and someone else by then. Talk of the highway assumes the present tense. The local paper runs a front-page piece on how to navigate a roundabout. The Sunday drive assumes proportions it never dreamed of. A *dual carriageway*. Could the term be any more charming, or less appropriate? And each time a new one opens, we shave minutes off the trip to Dublin. As if through some polite willingness on our part to illustrate a proof of plate tectonics, we inch ever closer to the capital.

THE OLD ROAD

Despite my love of speed and the queer way that vast, industrial swath through the scree appealed to me, when coming to you I stuck instead to the old road. With its bad bends, its fog banks, its stray cows come upon round corners and our own agreement that the new way was far less arduous, the old nevertheless maintained a coy hold on my loyalty. As though to remind me of where I'd come from, or of the condition in which I'd first arrived at your door. Slow and inefficient, knotted.

The old road bearing the weight and imprint of all those winter nights I travelled to and from you. Who I was, or who you were, on any given Friday. My stabs at perpetuity. My way of saying I'll keep returning to wherever you are, somehow the same, somehow fortified against change, against age and the flux of season and the occasional fit of pique. My way of knowing that we have been here, again and again, at your huge hearth at the end of each workweek, swapping laconically the details of our lives. Who you pined for, or who I did. Long-distance liaisons. Sound advice. Constancy and repetition and yet the bloom of things too. For laconic as we were, we were not immune to wonder, imagining we saw our very souls ripen under the watchful eyes of time and mutual regard.

HERE

At dawn or on summer evenings, the landscape an inversion of itself, things assuming their complementary colours: a yellow sky; Benbulben, which I know to be green, now a deep magenta. Five hundred twenty-six metres high and always there, in its uncanny self-possession, its horizontal thrust, its air of presumption and demand. Depending on the light, the angle, my own mood: priapic jut, or extended arm ushering me in, and northward. And to the south, its other: dome to its mantel, afloat while it is all full steam ahead. Self-satisfied, too, but afterwards, and in repose. Flat on its back and pooling like an ample breast.

PARKING DISCS

To the introduction of which nothing definitive could be attributed. Not the end of an era, not the mark of our entry into the grown-up world of cineplexes, bottle banks, espresso bars and, yes, the sex shop. But something. A kind of attrition.

In the beginning, we parked in cul-de-sacs or on the outskirts. Or we cheated – 'recycled' – carefully arranging on the dash hair squeegies, ballpoint pens or cigarette lighters over the already scratched squares of our tattered parking discs. We swapped tips on hidden spaces, as though they were undiscovered holiday destinations. (That private lot smack in the centre of town, some still-virgin corner of the world.) Gradually, though, we gave in. Learned to plan ahead. Bought in bulk packets of ten, and forgot there was ever a time when we didn't have to pay to park.

The papers say we are living in a boom town, and we feel it. We feel that weird, too-quick reversal of decay. And each time something picturesque and tumbledown vanishes and something baby blue or canary yellow or forest green rises in its place, we sense the presence of allegory. Allegory is among the words we don't much use here, but we know enough to know when it's among us. Each time we forget what once existed in any given place, we are visited by a vague unease, as though we have colluded in some dubious scientific advance.

BEFORE ...

and in the company of some other you. Platonic too, but with whom so many roles were played. Who's lost, who's found, first me, then you. So that I'm waiting, uneasily, for the next reversal. Or better yet, the final incarnation of us: some sync finally fallen into, a place (on the far shore) where suspicion's banished, ethanol extinct, and gratitude so deep-ingrained it isn't necessary to refer to.

That Christmas – our cold hands calcifying round our wine glasses in the icy studio of some mutual artist friend – we clung to one another in the corner like a pair of co-dependent limpets, guffawing over my latest half-remembered scrape, and you had the backhanded good grace to say to me: *There's a good woman going to loss in there.* Two years later, some early-morning stint in your place, the heebie-jeebies now a spectator sport to me, and I'm trying hard to say the same to you – a good man – because it's true. Because I never have, and still can't.

IARNRÓD ÉIREANN

In the bathroom on the Sligo–Dublin railway line, a sign telling us how to turn on the water in the hand basin has been tampered with, so as to form a new message – the demanding, unheralded art of negative graffiti. Whole words scratched out, one 's' artfully obscured, and what we're left with is an in-joke with a world-view attached. Think of here: the affection with which ineptitude is regarded, the irony with which piety is infused. When visiting from abroad, if short on time and desiring to grasp this place in a soundbite, you might start here: *To obtain water ... pray.*

WHICH BRINGS US TO BORN-AGAIN VIRGINS

A mini-movement growing up on the far side of the Atlantic: recant your past carnality, reclaim your prelapsarian self. A sort of sexual face-lift. This news courtesy of Radio Telefís Éireann, and relayed with all the ill-suppressed mirth that such American hokum incites. Some weeks later (also via RTÉ, though now with quizzicality in place of mirth), this news: that the Pioneers are offering a deal. Temperance, they've decided, can start anytime. Even here, it's not about never anymore. Just two years without a drink and you too can wear the pin, be, as it were, born again. The brands of innocence we consider worth regaining. A juxtaposing that helplessly invites reduction: *the difference between us is* ... that we dream of re-imagining our sex lives; you, of alcoholic chastity.

... AFTER

That I could hand to you – *a good man*, after all – the rebirth of wonder. The chastening effect of mental clarity, emotional acuity, keenness of sensation. Strictly *bona fide* fear. In a word (so hackneyed it hurts), sobriety. No longer awash in that amniotic fluid. See it shaken from you, like excess sea water upon emerging, the evolutionary being that is you heeding an unconscious call to a next echelon. Or your own tide out, brackishness receded, detritus exposed, the dropped hints of your life – *still there* – marking the way back. Equivocal treasures you'd glean then, ugly only to the untrained eye, like the bleached skulls we see on other people's mantels, prized beyond reason for reasons other than themselves.

My Christmas list for you: an undiluted consciousness, the prickliness and nettle-itch of fresh idea, pins and needles – this time – of boyish awe, the eager jump-start of each early morning, a mind you could strike a match on. If I could see it through sufficiently, to the point where I can say I haven't failed you. To the naff soda pops and the too-much smoking. To the living gingerly, the chaperoned existence, the life as though in kid gloves. To the graceful retirement of the antihero and the point of diminishing returns. Not only reached, but recognized.

NOW

In a parking lot somewhere in New Jersey, amidst a sea of stickered bumpers (declarations of intent, pithy quips, statements of preference), one-stop wisdom shop of the New World –

> *There are many vacancies in the motel of your mind.*
> *Handguns in schools: for or against?*
> And marvellously: *I'd rather be sailing to Byzantium*

– there in the land of mobility and reinvention, simulation and submerged rebirthing, alien abduction and impregnation, of wishful thinking never content to remain so, one radical assertion of intransigence stands out, a lone (ironic) voice sagely, trenchantly satisfied with its lot:

I'd rather be here, now.

HOME

Always when off the train. And at just that spot. Someone said it's hard to leave here because of that configuration of mountain and shoreline, the curvature of one along the other and the way we're lodged between. Concentric vortex of an embrace, poisoned chalice, gift tax.

But always on returning from the capital it hits, the bashfulness that too much generosity inspires. Summer evenings especially, coming west by train. Three hours of hell, then ... *Carrick-on-Shannon, Boyle, Ballymote, Collooney* ... and knowing it's coming, finding it there, stepping down onto the platform, a sort of guilty glee, as though I've skipped with the booty and this is it:

being here. That strangely subterranean feel to the place, to being this little bit beyond the pale and harbouring the secret of where a thing is hid.

Into the car then, down, down the hill and out of town, into the deepening quiet and the thickening dark, spelunking my way towards home. The same chagrin at my own dumb joy and just when I'm wondering what's behind it, it's there, in front of me, curving into view. That overly invoked mountain that two days ago I couldn't get shut of fast enough, over my shoulder everywhere I went, like a cheap dick on my tail, always *there*, in whatever ham disguise: pink, green, black, cut cake, 2-D cut-out, tidal wave, hung curtain, bad landscape painting, noun demanding adjectival range I haven't got. But now, seeing it afresh, I'm brought to heel, as corny as it feels. Just there. At Rathcormack, with the mountain on my right, the bay on my left, and that water-slide of a road, easing me into home. The plink of hit water. My own silent shout of delight.

... WELL AS WELL HIM AS ANOTHER ...

or so it pays to pretend. Until such time, anyway, as the clear truth of its antithesis can be admitted: that parts, while consecutive, are by no means interchangeable. That a hierarchy of affection exists – complete with petty power struggle, cut deal, bloodless coup, the tenterhook of dominion near-divested, and the pathos of the monarch unaware of plot-simmer – theocratic or despotic or with the mind-bending intricacy of the most bloated bureaucracy, but never, ever populist.

And always, long afterwards, the one we still talk about, the golden age of whatever our private civilization's been.

You? But could I ever know this before the end? Before all theory's been tested and each variable assigned value. The temptation to believe some untried proof remains.

If I'm even asking, it probably isn't you.

But your way of going on, like life was a game you'd deigned to play. Rather graciously, rather indulgently, all things considered (though granted, with an underlying gravity). Your figurative pose: winsomely awkward adult seated lotus-like in front of some board game with pretty coloured pieces and squares you can't afford to land on. Eager player, player by whatever wacky handed-down rules, consulter of box top when arbitrating chaos – kids' favourite bachelor uncle – but angling all the time to divine the grand design, the blackly comic hand of the creator (Milton-Bradley©) obvious to you at every turn. You've it sussed, you at your two levels, but to your credit aren't pretending you're not thoroughly engaged. Or that you don't know your place; fetch-ingly – as relatively in the dark as anyone – you aren't above avail-ing of kid-wisdom.

Some near-future, when I can take you with a grain of salt, stop concocting overblown metaphors for your existence. My fantasies now reduced to those of resignation, dead nerves, you having worn yourself thin. Once, though, it was like what I've heard of heroin: like being kissed by God. So I'm counting on the flat affect to follow. But that image won't hold up; your grip on me will loosen, after all. To the point where it's work to want you; already (sometimes), something more than simply waking is required. And after that – I hope – I'll find you there. But with-out the power to call up anything at all in me other than that old sardonic warmth. And I will wax eloquent for you on the matter of my latest object of desire, your by now banal presence remind-ing me that he – like you, like all my other little gods – will fall.

... ANOTHER

Our first touch, the coy plucking of insects off of one another's sleeves.

Oh, and you've one too. Here, let me ...

Days earlier, before we'd even spoken, I'd sat three rows behind you in a half-full theatre, imagining your hand through your hair was my own. Following your attention to where it wandered. Feeling cooler when you shed your coat. Smiling when you looked left to display, for my benefit, your profile. I thought I felt you squirm under the creaturely scent-sniff of my gaze and suddenly liked you, very much, for submitting so civilly to my inspection.

Later, when I referred to it, you surprised me by claiming that the whole mute exchange had been only in my mind. But I'm less convinced than ever. Your way of being, once I knew you, only confirming my suspicions. You were rare that way, how you could sit back and be enjoyed. Almost – I hate to say it – female, the way you gave yourself. Stealing the show like that: all object. I get it finally, the slavish love of beauty. The need to keep you in my sightline, and at my fingertips. The way, like an animal, I squirreled away sensations, stockpiling them for the cold spell to come.

LOVE AND MARRIAGE

In the kitchen of some too-long-married couple I know, I see they've retiled the walls. Over dinner, they conduct a tête-à-tête of injury and insult, the text from which they're working so highly allusive the rest of us can only hum along. We're all waiting for the split, for the relief of it. I, in fact, am betting they won't see next week. But then I think about their kitchen. The forward march of it. The things people do when we aren't around. Plugging away like that. Piling brick on brick. Surprising us with the way they keep rising from their deathbeds.

SOLIPSISM

Or a distant cousin of. Conundrum of unrequited love: that there is nothing so unlikely to arouse my sympathy or interest as your (unreciprocated) ardour for me. When what should please me more than passing hours in your company, pondering your unshakeable faith in my splendidness? Pining alongside you even, as we gaze into the near distance together, our four eyes trained on that superlative creature we've agreed is *I*. I – and I transformed by you like every other routine, workaday object when seen through your presently narcotized eyes – should be the sole subject of which I never tire.

So how is it instead that what I feel is pawed? I love you, after all, just not that way. How is it then that your own love sits between us like an intrusive third party? A crasher at our table, a morose drunk, a mourner who's so far exceeded the limits of our sympathy as to arouse resentment. Injecting into our otherwise gay little soirée the end of fun, a parental call to order, the killjoy knell of schoolbells, dawn. I watch, helplessly, as myself is extracted from myself. Yolk from white. Or decanted and given back to me as dregs, while you hold on to what's finest. You say I have 'taken possession' of you and yet it is I who feel owned. Where have I gone? And how can I give back to you the gift of indifference, the same indifference I once worked so hard to overcome?

Thankfully, this tells me something. That the anguish I myself am so enjoying (over someone other than you) will never – however stubbornly it tries – create something where there is nothing. This is how I'm able to believe what beggars belief: that while I have not for one full minute failed to think of him, or performed one interior monologue but for *him* to hear, or sat still *anywhere* but that I envisioned his smiling, inexplicable entrance (never mind the fact he's out of town, out of the country, has never heard of here, and doesn't drive anyway), I – like some out-of-the-way eatery he often forgets exists – have not even occurred to him tonight.

This is how I learn the necessity of giving up, through this grown-up game of Pass the Parcel.

'RAPTURE'

Which I first heard while sitting on your porch. That screened-in affair which seemed suspended in mid-air, the way it jutted out over a mini-valley, the path cut through the trees unfurling underneath us. The constant rain, the always saturated earth, the vertiginousness of our perch, and the delicate discordancy of *Thirteen Harmonies*.

We felt straight out of *Deliverance*.

Ice melting. Or that was what you called it. Falling apart, it felt like. And then later, watching, as I failed to fall apart.

I'm thinking of a scavenger hunt, a game I used to love, and the list I'd need to help me find you: John Cage, Dusty Springfield, the Ford dealership on 202, resourcefulness, your own love of lists, that shade of blue, your spot-on send-up of the Stage Manager in *Our Town*, the library and the field beside – alive each night with lightning bugs, living by your wits, your own regained wonder (after the 'intervening years of anaesthetization'), bicycles, Bonnard, a sleek black lap-top, and 1:26 of 'Rapture'.

CHRISTMAS

Dinner and a long walk through Dromahair. Blatantly storybook, with winding lane, lone spire perforating mist, duskiness congealing too quickly into night, and we seven – gloved and hatted – trudging smally through the stock-still hills. Barnacle geese in the marshy field, wintering here before their spring coupling else-where. And of humans? All with me in pairs, all six snug aboard the ark. Sweet platonic friendships I could frankly do without; company, under the circumstances, always worse than solitude. At home, at least, I've my familiars – undemanding silence, ritual of book and bed, arch-backed animal rising sleepily at the sound of my key turning – sticks to beat self-pity down. Self-pity, that ravenous ingrate that rises balefully at the simple act of 'bucking up' for company. Uninvited guest grossly feeding on itself. Asex-ual reproducer gone berserk, begetting and begetting with no apparent need for outside intervention (though the hospitality of friends will do nicely). Touch Socratic even, in its arrogance, how it runs rings round what I'm absolutely sure is reason.

But there's no reasoning with now. This time of year is cruel, and makes glaring all our lacks. You gone by then, and like a ghost beside me. You are anyone by now, though, and what's glaring is your very lack of specificity. An absence generic as a presence never could be, though on the side of each this much could be said: if present, possibility personified; if absent, failure of same.

This year's lesson: that loneliness, like a sick cell, will reinvent itself. Mutate, strengthen, grow resistant to the old remedies. That there are strains I haven't even dreamed of.

INCANTATION,
prayer at bedtime, Angelus for the secular set.

From Malin Head to Howth Head to the Irish Sea.

Swaddled in my bed, quick listen to the news, just before lights out, just checking: was there anything that happened I should know about?

From Carnsore Point to Valentia to Erris Head.

Sudden sense of smallness, shelter and inclusion. The fact

that weather can be met, across the board, with only silence. Incongruous comfort of our collective ineffectuality – the few limits we do share. Why winter has always seemed the most communal of seasons. How death stymies – then binds – the living, levelling who's left as well.

From Erris Head to Belfast Lough to Hook Head.

Quiet pang of guilt. For what? For being here. Cosseted by airwaves, by four walls from the audible wind, warm, dry, safe and, really, OK. For the dumb good luck then of being here, which on the best days seems surely a remarkable omission, or oversight.

Rosslare. Roche's Point Automatic. Valentia. Belmullet ... 999 steady ... 996 and rising slowly ... Loop Head. Mizen Head. Carnsore Point. And on the Irish Sea.

Never more foreign than now. And yet, on hearing, of all things, the Sea Area Forecast, never since a child this tucked-in sensation. Crack of light under the door and life going on beyond it. Someone out there, with an eye on things. Parameters delineated. The compass-points of home. To be told where I am, and what bound by. Like the child's incantation. Universe: galaxy: solar system: planet: hemisphere: continent: nation: state: city: street ...

... H O M E

Out the back, a biopsy of *here*. Field, hill and dale. Copse, the spire at Lissadell, hunkered shrubs cordoning off holdings, red-roofed barns and one stark white bungalow. The mountain – robbed at twilight of its contours – now a prow on the horizon. Through the keyhole view I'm given – this lens eye – pan here, then here, pull back, wide angle now, see a country echo in concentric rings of just this. Or fly over it. All like a doll's house, down to diminutive detail, and knowable, you think, in one crossing. The human scale of things. The illusion therefore that you can grasp it. Learn the one thing you need to live here.

TOURISM

Moon over the back sheds on ink-blue nights. A rusty bike and wagon wheel propped against the side stone wall. The sheds, just shells of things. You see them everywhere. Candidates for conversion. But I like them roofless. The way the gable ends stand, regardless, as if holding up their end of the bargain. Every so often – out of the blue and never when I seek the thrill – it broadsides me, this scene in silhouette. I stare, like a tourist, into relative prehistory.

And you, living in the shadow of that old abbey. When I'd asked and you'd told me – *1508*, offhandedly – I was silenced. Centuries still strike me dumb, no matter what I learn, just keep seeming beyond my ken. As though I'm all jig time, quik-stop, planned obsolescence. What's coming, rather than what's gone.

Constellations, first here, now here. The stars obscured for weeks by cloud cover and suddenly it breaks, and like the automated flick from one slide in the carousel to the next: a new view. Over and over, the strobing of the night sky. I step outside before bed and look up. Sometimes, even on the clearest nights: *nothing*: my own laziness of heart. A guilty inability to rise to the occasion. Sometimes, though, an awe that seems almost equal to the sight. A wholeness and no complaint. The *knowing*. And the not fearing not knowing.

THE HALE-BOPP

Zany name for what hung over us that summer, as though to keep us from taking miracle too seriously. Sounding to me like a dance my mother might have done forty-some years ago. Jiving at a mixer in West Philly. It used to hover, suspended dead centre above the straight stretch of the Donegal Road. And I, driving north, each time with the illusion of drawing nearer to it.

You then too. There with me and eye trained skyward, you. Not another, not yet fallen nor ever will be. But with me. Two of us then, standing, with our simple mouths agape and my heart gone out to us. In that prolonged instant of afforded joy, in which the eye-blink of wish-time was arrested. When we stood, you and I there, in a state of continuous grace, under that one always falling star which finally, that September, fell from view.